A PENSION FOR DEATH

By the same author

A Cracking of Spines
The Manuscript Murders

A PENSION FOR DEATH

Roy Harley Lewis

St. Martin's Press
New York

For information, address St. Martin's Press, 175 Fifth Avenue, New York, N.Y. 10010.

Library of Congress Cataloging in Publication Data

Lewis, Roy Harley.
A pension for death.

I. Title.
PR6062.E9543P4 1983 823'.914 83-2888
ISBN 0-312-60004-6

First U.S. Edition

10 9 8 7 6 5 4 3 2 1

First published in Great Britain by Robert Hale Limited.

One

Always the perfect host, he stifled a yawn. Not that he was in any way bored; on the contrary, it had been surprisingly pleasant. It seemed they had far more in common than he had been led to suppose. The meeting had been the outcome of a business proposition that was intriguing, as well as novel. Involving, admittedly, a greater degree of speculation than investments more familiar to him, it nevertheless offered considerably higher returns. Even the risk factor could be entertaining.

The negotiations had provided a welcome change from the customary dry-as-dust clinical evaluation of statistics, and since the mood was friendly they had taken drinks during as well as after the discussion. Out of respect for his guest he had made it clear well before the end that he would have to decline the offer to participate – but such was the degree of bonhomie that it had been taken in good part.

His visitor's bottle of malt whisky, although incredibly expensive, was not really to his taste but it would have been ungracious to have commented; and, in any case it was his palate that was probably at fault – no doubt ruined by imbibing the same brand year in, year out. It was stronger too, because after only three doubles he was uncharacteristically tired. No, *pleasantly relaxed*, he assured himself. Yet he had to grit his teeth to prevent another yawn, and knew that he needed to distract his companion ... get up and *do* something ... a dip in the pool perhaps? He remembered the swimming-pool had not been heated, and the prospect of even the slightest sudden chill was daunting. The *jacuzzi* was different. He had paid a small fortune to have the damned thing installed, so he used it as often as possible, and automatically switched the heating on whenever he came into the house. There was nothing better for relaxing and being toned up at the same time.

It was reasonable to suppose that his guest might enjoy a break; they had been talking for more than an hour. There was a range of swimming-costumes for guests of both sexes – although invariably he tried to persuade the ladies that one had to be completely naked to get the best from a jacuzzi – so the suggestion was quite practical. He did not bother to conceal the yawn this time; indeed, he made a feature of it as the excuse for a dip.

As he had anticipated, the offer was welcomed so there was no longer any need to put on an act. Dispensing with his usual "sales" talk about the "restorative" features of the jacuzzi, he got undressed quickly to give himself up to the warmly seductive embrace of the caressing jets of water. Normally, he would have resisted the temptation to leap in – to wait for the other person to precede him – but the tiredness overwhelmed his customary good manners.

It was the tremendous relief he knew it would be, yet after the initial surge of excitement the effect was something of an anticlimax – he did not feel any less tired than before. In fact, he began to feel apprehensive that if he did not get a grip on his senses he was in danger of dozing off. The concern was not helped by his companion's tardiness, even now making some lame excuse to disappear – something about going to the toilet. Despite the mild irritation, he smiled. How respectable. What was the point of paying for an expensive filtering system if it did not enable one to do the sensible thing – and to hell with convention? The irritation returned ... if his guest did not appear soon he would have to think about getting out, because the languor had become quite oppressive.

There was little chance of drowning, of course. The instant his head dipped below the surface, the shock would surely wake him ... unless ... what if it was more than tiredness? What if he was ill? The realisation made his stomach heave. It seemed obvious now ... the tiredness was so overpowering that he might have been drugged and, since that was out of the question, the evidence pointed to what he had long dreaded – the onset of a critical illness. This could be the overdue penalty for burning the candle at both ends. Despite the weight over his eyes, his mind was quite detached as though he had been given the power to diagnose his own condition. He could tell, for example, that since there was no pain in his chest, it was not a heart attack. Logically, he reasoned, it must be a stroke, hopefully only slight.

He made a tremendous effort to climb out of the water, but his limbs disobeyed the command, and he was consciously reluctant to exert any more pressure on his brain in case in the circumstances he was doing the wrong thing. It was essential to remain calm, and by not moving he should be all right until help arrived. Where on earth was his guest? It was becoming an effort to hang on to the side of the jacuzzi; even to keep his eyes open.

He was on the point of calling for help when to his enormous relief he heard footsteps outside and a rather strange squeaking noise as the door opened.

Despite his anguished state he still hesitated over making a drama about the silly business and did not call out – hoping that the expression on his face was self-explanatory. But his good manners were wasted because his guest was too intent on manoeuvring in a cumbersome trolley on four rebelliously independent wheels, to pay any attention to him. On the trolley ... which usually came from the dining-room ... was a huge fish-tank he had never seen before. The sight was so incongruous that for a moment he forgot how ill he felt and gazed, transfixed, as the tank was tilted over the side of the trolley, its contents splashing into the jacuzzi.

The sick man wondered for a moment if he was hallucinating. From the way the ceiling lights caught the silvery scales, it seemed that the tank had contained tropical fish of some sort, although in his befuddled state he could not decide whether it was a practical joke in bad taste, or his guest's well-intentioned idea of a gift. Either way it was regrettable because goldfish, or whatever they were, had to be fed, and the filtering system was not designed to cope with that sort of unforeseen complication. The small circular shapes – dozens and dozens, it seemed – plopped into the water apparently as doped as he was. He was not an expert but it was obvious that they had not travelled well ... water too cold, perhaps, or not enough oxygen ... that was *all* he needed – dying fish to foul up the water!

However, the mischief had already been done, and he felt too ill to make a scene. It was better to say nothing and simply get rid of the fish when his guest left, even if it meant the bother of changing the water. He attempted a smile as the instigator of this madness came towards him, incredibly managing not to notice his anguished state.

The sick man tried to lift a hand out of the water but it was beyond him. He was barely aware of a hand above reaching towards him, presumably to haul him out, although nothing seemed to happen. Instead, he felt a stinging scratch at the back of his thigh.

Instinctively he tried to put a hand to the injured limb, but again the effort was too much. He looked down helplessly ... and there was blood in the water. Amazingly, his leg was bleeding. He looked accusingly at the figure above him, and his gaze was held fast, as though magnetized, by the razor-blade that protruded from the sensitive fingers.

He looked down again, bemused, at the redness of the water behind him, yet despite the preoccupation with blood he was conscious of the fish coming to life. About six-nine inches long, they were like children's imaginative drawings, short and round, silvery grey in colour with reddish underbelly. Then he felt another stinging scratch – no, it was a *bite* – near the original wound and looked down in irritation tinged with panic at the fish his blood seemed to have attracted; he had never seen fish as aggressive as this before. A second, a third and then *dozens* seemed to surround him almost simultaneously, jockeying for position as in turn they were buffeted by the jacuzzi's animated water jets. But they were persistent, and almost at once there was a multiplying rash of bites on both legs.

Suddenly, one of his attackers leapt out of the water and clamped its razor-sharp teeth on to his exposed forearm. It seemed all head and teeth, and virtually no body. Frantically, he tried to brush it off with his free hand and when it fell away again it was with a small strip of flesh. Actually *seeing* was something different ... a nightmare ... and he screamed in terror. He knew now that the fish attacking him were piranhas, forty or fifty of them at least.

The water in the jacuzzi looked like a corked *vin rosé*. Desperately he called for help, and the person above, sickened by the bloodletting, looked away. There was a helpless apology: "I miscalculated ... you were supposed to be unconscious by the time they ... "

The voice trailed off because the man in the water was no longer listening. Unable to stand on lacerated stumps, he overbalanced on to his back, inviting a fresh assault. From then on the watcher did not know whether the threshing limbs indicated a remaining element of life, or were merely the mechanical spasms that occur after death. Such thoughts had to be purged; there was no time to waste. It was doubtful whether the piranhas could finish such a massive meal, but meanwhile the pool had to be drained and cleaned and the water replaced – several times. There was at least a couple of hours hard work before the jacuzzi looked as enticing as it had before ... that is, a place for fun and games.

Two

The ten-foot-high wrought-iron gates and the tarmacadam drive, unwinding like a roll of lush black carpet into the distance, were impressive. But the sheer elegance of the 20-bedroom house built by Thomas Cubitt in 1824 took my breath away. It seemed almost indecent that Longlands, set majestically in 25 acres of Sussex parkland, with its trout stream and ornamental lake, should not belong to the nation so that its beauty could be shared.

The picture almost dispelled my ill humour and it was not until we had been met at the front door and given a lightning tour of the house – more like members of a coach party than guests – that the misgivings returned. For the umpteenth time I began to regret a Saturday spent away from the shop where I had promised to rearrange the bookcases to make room for an enlarged antiquarian section.

If any one thing epitomised the artificiality of the world into which we had emerged, it was the oversized jacuzzi with a huge tree planted in its middle so that the foliage disappeared into the roof. I stared at Laura reproachfully; it was she who had twisted my arm, making me lose sight of my priorities.

We were greeted by our host, Anthony Longstaff, with a beautiful woman he chose not to introduce, and I cannot deny that his handshake had been warm and his smile disarming. Yet almost at once I felt a quite unreasonable dislike for the philistines who had almost destroyed the character of the lovely house. What Longstaff did with his country home was no business of mine, and there is nothing wrong with a jacuzzi if you've got money to burn (because that is what the heating bills represent), but its size and the overpowering hot-house decor had turned a functional installation into a showbiz gimmick. Indeed, when Laura and I walked in, it is difficult to recall whether it was the fantasy setting that struck us first, or the three topless beauties self-consciously skylarking about on cue whenever a newcomer arrived.

I suppose my wandering eye is as agile as most, and perhaps because I am in my middle 30s and wary of approaching middle-age, there could even be a tendency to overcompensate, but in comparison with my companion, Laura Cottingham, the bathers looked what they were – tarts. What they were doing at Longlands was not difficult to imagine, although what the apparently absent Mrs Longstaff would make of it was more intriguing. With the hindsight of fully five minutes' acquaintanceship, Anthony Longstaff seemed to me more like a playboy or man-about-town than an actuary, yet Laura had told me that he was one of the most respected financial brains in London's business world.

Perhaps it was the relaxed air of success that I disliked; perhaps his indifference to my feelings as he laid siege to Laura. Like a child with a new toy, he was totally preoccupied. He may have been spoilt, but it was obvious to anyone that Laura was a rare specimen. Intelligent as well as beautiful, she was successful in her career, and independent. And if I seemed to be part of her life, then that was merely an added challenge.

You will gather, from the effect it had on me, that Laura and I are very close. The fact that we were not married was probably my fault; in ducking the final commitment. I tended to take her for granted. Yet when potential rivals threw down the gauntlet I was never as confident as I appeared.

The separate swimming-pool, the squash court and the sauna were the trappings of success, and if Longstaff was nearly twenty years older than me he was still immature enough to delight in showing them off – something else which rubbed me up the wrong way. I cannot stand show-offs. I concede that Longstaff might have countered that accusation by pointing out that *I* didn't have much to show off anyway – which is true. Furthermore, in a more rational frame of mind I would have to admit that there was little difference between his pride in his possessions and mine in my antiquarian bookshop.

Perhaps not. I do myself an injustice. The bookshop, part of a Queen Anne house at Ardley in Dorset is unquestionably beautiful, but I have never tried to pretend it was my creation. The oak beams and the restored original fireplace were there long before I arrived on the scene. It was my predecessor who gave the shop its character, although inevitably I had added touches of my own, such as the antique weaponry – the swords and muskets – that alongside some fine old copper bedwarmers decorated the limited space between bookshelves.

But if I'm rattling on like a professional guide I apologise, because it is the books – more than 20,000 of them – that spill over into every nook and cranny that makes the place such a delight, attracting bibliophiles from all over the country, as well as many of my postal customers from abroad who look me up when they are over for a visit, despite the distance from London.

So, you'll gather from all this that I'm also a hypocrite – every bit as proud as Longstaff, and jealous in the bargain, at least when we were competing for Laura's attention. If you are wondering why, in such a belligerent mood, I deigned to accept the man's hospitality, I've just asked myself the same question, and the answer is embarrassing. The object of the exercise was to sell Longstaff a few books. Not for himself – I don't suppose he ever had time to read, or the inclination – but as a potentially promising business arrangement.

It had been Laura's idea. Longstaff worked for Allman & Spinks (GB), the second largest drugs conglomerate in Europe – although in terms of profitability the UK operation was usually headed by the sister companies in Germany and Switzerland. To say that Longstaff worked for the company is almost to give the wrong impression. He was an employee only in the sense that the company still paid his national insurance. In all other respects he was his own master. He was in charge of the group's substantial pension fund and therefore independent of the normal business machine. His talents were so specialised that he was given a completely free hand. It meant that he earned almost as much as the group chairman, but since he was in effect a consultant there were few of the responsibilities.

As an actuary, Longstaff was originally concerned with applying the theory of probability, primarily in relation to life assurance. In those early days he was responsible for fixing premiums and valuing liabilities, and his calculations were faultless. But it was not until he was given the authority to administer the pension funds investments that he really came into his own, and his value to the company could be measured in millions. Longstaff found himself blessed with an instinctive judgement, or *flair* – a quality he had hitherto distrusted – which, linked to the computer that passed for his brain, seemed incapable of error. Within a few years his annual spending, i.e. the investment budget, had risen nearly 100% to £80 million. With this success, so his personality began to blossom. Relatively late in life, he began to make use of the fortune he was acquiring. Now, with a lovely wife, and a stately country home, he was still gripped by a determination to make up for lost time.

Laura was a partner in the top London agency that handled Allman & Spink's corporate advertising programme, and since she was concerned with the group's "image" she was on friendly terms with several members of the board. Longstaff worked hard to develop that relationship.

In his early fifties, he had developed a fetish about diet and fitness, and it showed. A couple of inches taller than my six feet, he was thin – barely 150 lbs – but it suited him, and his aristocratic face was unlined. His curly hair was still quite thick and tinted a distinguished grey at the temples – so neatly, in fact, that it might have been applied from a bottle; although I suspect my judgement in that respect is not entirely dispassionate. In short, he was a good-looking man of the world, sophisticated, and above all rich enough to enjoy a life-style I would never know. Even his monogrammed pyjamas were made by the most exclusive tailors in Savile Row.

Longstaff's seduction of beautiful women – a campaign launched less than ten years ago – was successful enough to jade the palate. It had become almost a formality so that when Laura kept the relationship on a business footing, at first he suspected she was playing him at his own game. But invitations to Longlands continued to be deflected until he began to lose his composure. Until, one day at a company reception where he had been telling members of the board of his plans to broaden the scope of his investment portfolio, Laura saw an opportunity to help me. It seemed that while something like 96% of the pension funds would still be channelled into traditional outlets – land, property and industrial investment – he had set aside about 4% for what he called "fringe" areas, such as paintings, antiques and antiquarian books.

Laura had pricked up her ears, having often heard me sounding off about books for investment – except that I was usually *complaining* about people who bought rare books as an investment without any interest in what they were buying; some who even kept them unseen in a safe deposit. But Laura kept to my "vast" knowledge, my reputation and links with the Antiquarian Booksellers Association. Of course, she failed to mention that my links with the "top" end of the trade were coincidental; that my expertise in other spheres had foisted on me the role of sheriff without a badge; but then I suppose I should not grumble that she was a good salesman.

The result was a pleasant 50-mile drive through the network of unspoilt secondary roads that linked the three counties – and my first meeting with the man I had heard so much about. Now that Longstaff had Laura on his home ground, the last thing he wanted to do was to talk business with me. To complicate matters I'm not a natural salesman. I deal in old books because I like them and enjoy meeting people who share my interests, so that I was not enthusiastic at the prospect of talking business to someone whose mind was clearly elsewhere. Fortunately for my bank balance there is also a streak of obstinacy that baulked at the inclination to stand on my dignity. If Longstaff had fixed the appointment merely to please Laura, then let him fulfil his obligation. I grasped the nettle when Laura went off to change into her swimming-costume. Longstaff politely excused himself, but I cut off his retreat, reminding him why I was there.

"This is probably not the best time to discuss books," I conceded, "but perhaps we can establish if there is any common ground? If what Laura told me is accurate – that you need someone to put together a portfolio of rare books, then I think I can help. If that is a basis for discussion perhaps we could meet again at your office more formally?"

I could see from the glazed look in his eyes that he had not given the matter much thought. He nodded vaguely. "There isn't really much to discuss," he said, "It's a new market as far as we are concerned. We need an expert we can trust. Laura says we couldn't find anyone better."

I smiled. "That's more than a slight exaggeration..."

He looked surprised at my frankness but still not terribly interested and, when his eyes lit up, I followed the direction of his gaze, becoming aware of the approach of a young woman. Judging from the way she was dressed, she had been riding. With long blond hair drawn back from her face in a pony-tail, she looked very young, probably not more than her late teens, but there was nothing unsophisticated about her eyes. As she joined us I noticed there was a fine film of perspiration on her face, and that the thin cotton of a man's check shirt was damp with sweat and stuck to her body. Since the shirt was unbuttoned almost to the waist and she was obviously wearing no bra, the picture was disconcerting and I felt my adrenalin beginning to stir. I could see I was not the only one affected and Longstaff's expression held a mixture of affection and lust. Apparently indifferent to me she kissed him on the mouth and he put an arm around her possessively.

So much for the absent Laura, I thought.

"Tony, there are a couple of broken slats on the wooden bridge across the stream. It could be dangerous ... "

"All right, darling. I'll report it later." Then he remembered me. "Matthew Coll, I'd like you to meet Jacintha ... Jacintha Farini ... "

We shook hands.

"Jacintha is my stepdaughter."

I tried to keep my face expressionless, although on reflection I might have been less surprised had she been his real daughter. There was a strong sexual aura about the girl that seemed to match his, although he had the years and the experience to disguise it.

"I'm sweating like a pig. I'm going to take a shower and then cool off in the pool," she announced, talking to Longstaff but her eyes on me. "Do you have some trunks with you?"

I nodded. "I'll probably come in later. Your stepfather and I were just talking business ... "

She pulled a face. The sulky eyes gave her an air of petulance and I was mesmerized by the full lower lip.

"For a moment I thought you were one of the film people Tony has started to cultivate. You look too rugged to be one of his cronies from the City."

"Matt is a bookseller," Longstaff interrupted. "I'm consulting him about buying some rare books."

"Oh?" Surprisingly there was a modicum of interest in her tone. "Then you must know Frensham's in Grosvenor Square. They're the best, I'm told. Royal appointments and all those things."

"One of the best," I conceded. "I do know them." I saw no point in adding that Wilfred Frensham, chairman of the old-established London firm, and a past president of the A.B.A, was a good friend of mine. When I first came into the business, Frensham had recruited my services in tracking down the gang responsible for a series of thefts from shops and libraries*. He had since been helpful to me in practical ways.

* *A Cracking of Spines*

"Some of them are a bit fuddy-duddy," she continued, "but I know the chap who really runs the place ... "

"Oh?"

"Hugo Diringer. You must have heard of him. I'd be pleased to introduce you."

Diringer was a personable young man in his late twenties, probably a future director of the company, but for the moment a relatively unimportant member of the staff who had no doubt impressed Jacintha by his good looks and "blue" blood. However, I had no quarrel with him and nodded politely.

Laura rejoined us, striking in a plain green one-piece costume that cunningly set off her auburn hair and green eyes to perfection. Even Jacintha looked impressed when Longstaff, hastily withdrawing his hand from her waist, introduced them. Whether her only concern was to promote my cause, or whether for some reason she wanted to score a point off the younger girl, Laura butted into our conversation with a surprising lack of subtlety, "Isn't Dillinger, or whatever his name is, one of the poor devils you outbid when you got the Lanier manuscript* at auction?" Without waiting for my response she turned to Longstaff. "What did I tell you?"

Longstaff said nothing but raised an appreciative eyebrow, and suddenly I felt embarrassed at accepting congratulations that were barely justified. "Frensham's were speculating with their own money; I was merely representing an American university ... "

A shadow of annoyance flitted across Laura's face and she cut me short: "We were talking about judgement!" My heart warmed towards her and I

* *The Manuscript Murders*

could not help squeezing her arm reassuringly.

Unaware of the relationship, Jacintha continued to dangle what she assumed was the right bait. "I'm in London most of the time. I must look you up ... "

To be completely frank, since Laura and I lived and worked more than 100 miles apart, which means that we saw each other infrequently, I might have been flattered by a visit from someone as unusual as Jacintha, but it was not to be. "My shop is at Ardley in Dorset," I explained. "I'm afraid I'm just a country bookseller."

The picture dispelled any romantic notions she might have entertained. Frensham's elegant gallery in Mayfair was so august and imposing that the staff seemed a cut above even its titled customers. To people like Jacintha, with her limited perspective, Hugo did not give the impression of working. He merely dabbled in rare and beautiful books between winter sports in Austria and the Diringer family villa in Monaco. In contrast, running a shop in a not especially fashionable market town put me in the category of local trademan. Laura had called me a country bumpkin as a term of endearment, but it was obvious that Jacintha was no democrat. There was an embarrassed silence for a moment before she asked: "The yellow Citroen round by the side of the house ... is that yours?"

I nodded. I was proud of my GSU Club with its finely tuned engine, but I could see what she was getting at. It was the odd car out in an eye-catching collection of Ferraris, Aston Martins, Jags and BMWs; and it confirmed her fears that she had been wasting her time.

"Well," she announced brightly, cutting her losses. "My shower awaits."

Rather to my surprise, Longstaff seemed embarrassed, and although he did not comment on her hasty departure he gave the impression of wanting to make amends. "We were talking about books when the child came in ... You were saying ... ?"

Whatever my earlier impression, there was no denying he had good manners. " ... that perhaps we could fix a meeting at your office?"

"Of course. But meanwhile since you've taken the trouble to drive here today let's sort out the principles first. We'll go in the library ... "

Laura excused herself and headed for the pool while Longstaff led the way to what was for me the surprise of the day. In keeping with the hasty image I had formed, I imagined a snooker room "decorated" by shelves lined with sumptious leather bindings bought by the yard as "fittings", all of them unread. Instead I found a large but quite cosy room, richly carpeted, and with wall-to-wall grey velvet curtains at one end, open at that time of day and with a view across the terrace of undulating parkland. It was sparsely furnished; from memory there were just three old and obviously comfortable leather armchairs and an enchanting writing-table – it looked like Chippendale, although I am not an expert on furniture. On the three sides there were shelves filled with books of all shapes and sizes, a few in leather but mainly in cloth and some even in paperback.

Longstaff laughed at my surprise. "It's my wife's room. You'd obviously have more in common with her. Unfortunately Ellen is staying at the London flat tonight. She goes to the theatre a lot, and I don't like her to drive all this way back at night."

I had heard of Ellen Longstaff, a divorcee he had married little more than six years earlier. She was younger than him by ten years, and despite their vastly different backgrounds, and (it seemed) their different interests, it was rumoured to be a love-match. However, the topless girls in the jacuzzi, Longstaff's obvious affection for his stepdaughter, and the frequent nights spent apart, indicated to me that the marriage was – or had become – one of convenience.

He waved me to a seat and poured me a generous measure of Old Grouse whisky. It was new to me. I said I liked it and he smiled appreciatively as though we did have something in common at last. "It's the only brand I drink from choice." He helped himself and took an armchair facing me.

"What do you know about my business?" he began.

"Very little. I know your company employs many thousands of people, and that they pay a proportion of their wages into a pension fund which provides them with an annuity on retirement. It's your job to invest that money to the maximuum advantage."

"Something like that."

"And I imagine a little more sophisticated than buying national savings certificates?"

" … Or gambling on the stock exchange. The risk factor is what it's all about. Experienced colleagues of mine have come unstuck on what seemed to be the safest bets, lulled into a sense of false security by the apparent respectability of a venture. My reputation has been built on accepting gamblers' odds, but without the gamble … "

"So I've heard."

"Then you've also heard that a couple of years ago I started to diversify. It was becoming boring. So instead of keeping all our eggs in one basket we started looking for other outlets – and we bought our first Old Master. Inevitably, our success at the Turner sale last year made the national press, but it also meant that my rivals jumped on the bandwaggon. Now I want to get in first with rare books. People have been talking about it for years but as far as I know, no-one has actually put his money where his mouth is – at least, not on the scale I'm talking about."

"It is surprising no-one has actually taken the plunge," I agreed. "The Economist Intelligence Unit did a fascinating survey a few years ago. They took a 20-year period and did an analysis of gains and losses on a couple of hundred transactions in pictures, books and *objets d'art* – compared with stocks offered in the City or on Wall Street. Books and modern paintings came out on top of the table."

"I remember seeing it just after buying our Turner, and being rather disturbed that Old Masters – as opposed to modern paintings – didn't show too well."

"You've probably spent more time analysing the figures than people in the book trade."

"Percentages and statistics are my job. I got my assistant to do a computer analysis of *Book Auction Records* for the past 25 years, so that we could draw certain conclusions. I can remember some of the more spectacular increases even now – months later. But that doesn't make me an expert on books, what to buy ... or how much. I've got into the habit of not going to market until the last piece of the jigsaw fits into place – and that means an expert on the team."

"You realise of course, that there are very few books that would fetch as much as the paintings you've been buying. You might have to pay around £1 million for a Gutenberg bible, but the chances of finding one for sale are pretty remote. Presumably you're prepared to lower your sights?"

"Considerably. Our researches show that the most

impressive gains are among books under £500, but since we're not about to buy them by the ton, obviously a compromise is called for. On the other hand, for the reasons I've given I would prefer this to be a low-key operation."

I nodded. "That will mean staying away from the big auctions – which saves money for a start; auctions are sometimes convenient, but the dearest way to buy. It's preferable to shop around ... that way one can find bargains ... "

"We're not looking for bargains – just books that will appreciate over a ten-twenty-year period, actually keeping ahead of the stockmarket and some of our other investments."

"No problem. Obviously there is an element of swings and roundabouts, but I can come up with a portfolio that satisfies your requirements. What sort of figure are we talking about? £50,000?"

"I was thinking of more like £300,000."

My jaw must have dropped and he quickly added: "My total budget this year is £80 million."

"I don't doubt you know what you're doing. You took my breath away because I'm not used to dealing on that scale. *My* annual budget – leaving out occasional big buys at auction for institutional clients abroad, which have a separate entry in my books anyway – is not much more than a third of that ... "

"Does it scare you?"

I studied him carefully. The question might have been offensive, but I could detect no hint of mockery. "No. But you're venturing a lot of money; are you certain you've got the right man for the job? Or indeed, why restrict yourself to any one person? Why not approach half a dozen of the top firms – dealers like Frenshams, the firm your stepdaughter mentioned, Quaritch or Maggs – and let us share the cake?"

"For two reasons. One: the fewer people who know about my plans the better. Secondly, I don't want anyone doubling or trebling their profit margin because they feel I'm not short of a bob or two ... " He raised a hand to forestall my protest. "Let's just say I would prefer to pay the most competitive prices; and there's nothing more competitive than trade price – which is what you would have to pay. Finally, by sharing out the cake as you put it, at the end of the day there is not much incentive for the Frenshams of this world. For you it's different. You see, we intend to pay a reasonable commission to the man who knows what he's doing. In return for the equivalent of five or six weeks work in a year, we're talking about a consultancy fee of £45,000 ... net profit."

Three

Money had never been an important consideration in my career. I enjoyed dealing in old books and, provided I could earn a reasonable living, there was little incentive to hunt for the crock of gold at the end of the rainbow. In theory "progress" in the book trade meant either a bigger shop in a major city – with all the additional headaches of unreliable staff and bureaucratic red tape that clogs the wheels of business these days – or to specialise in very rare books where the profit margins were so fat that one might need only to sell a half-dozen volumes a year to provide a lucrative income. Neither appealed. I had, after all, already opted out of the London rat race, to fall in love with Ardley – and my tiny corner of it in particular. Furthermore, one of the attractions of the kind of bookselling I had chosen was meeting people who share similar interests.

Much to my relief, Laura had declined the invitation for us to stay the night and Sunday at Longlands, and during the drive back to Dorset I tried to come to terms with the prospect of sudden wealth. What would I do with it? Despite Jacintha's reaction I did not want to change the car; I had no desire to take an expensive holiday, at least not in the foreseeable future; and the option of investing in additional stock while sensible was surely something of an anticlimax?

The conversation was sporadic because I continued to be preoccupied with what to most people was scarcely a problem. Luckily my relationship with Laura was such that both of us knew instinctively when the other was not in the mood for conversation. The thought reminded me of the warmth of my feelings towards her and I took my hand off the gear-stick to squeeze her thigh affectionately. Roused from daydreams of her own, she looked at me in surprise, curious about my motive. Grinning sheepishly, I protested: "You're always accusing me of being undemonstrative!"

It occurred to me at that moment there was one significant difference the impending income from Allman & Spinks might make – I could now afford to keep Laura in the manner – if you'll pardon the cliché – to which she was accustomed. My heart started to pick up speed with apprehension. Was this the time to pop the question? The anxiety was not all that surprising. There was no doubt that Laura *would* marry me ... the question was: on what terms? The last time we had spoken seriously about the future she had given the impression that while she understood my reasons for leaving London, she suspected it was a passing phase; that I was too young to bury myself in the country. Meanwhile, I had the same respect for her personal ambitions and did not see how they could be reconciled with pulling up firmly established roots and moving to Ardley. My heartbeats slowed to normal ... the big decision would have to be postponed.

With the pressure eased again, it dawned on me that I was counting my chickens over the impending jump in my standard of living. All I had was an expression of interest and possible intent, which was a long way from a contract. I asked Laura if she thought Longstaff could be trusted.

"What is there to trust?"

I shrugged. "It seems too good to be true ... Good fortune falling into my lap just like that ... "

"You'd rather sweat for it? If I did a checklist of the agency's clients, I'd say that we landed the majority of them with the minimum fuss. If the chase goes into months or even years, which sometimes happens, the chances are that they are leading you a dance."

"Okay. I concede that he met me today as a favour to you, but if he is as good at his job as his reputation suggests, I can't see him hedging business bets for personal considerations. He could go to *anyone* in the trade. Wilfred Frensham would welcome him with open arms ... "

"Wilfred would welcome *me* with open arms but I haven't been tempted yet either. I agree that Tony would not allow sentiment or even lust to influence his business judgement – but that merely confirms my impression that he thinks you can do the job he wants ..."

"What he wants," I echoed. "That's the 64-dollar question."

"You've lost me ... "

"Look, we know I'm a good bookseller; at least, in the league I'm competing in. With more experience I can only get better. But Wilfred has forgotten more about *rare* books than I'll ever know. The information I need to look up in reference books, he has stored in his head. Now if Longstaff can turn a blind eye to that sort of expertise I'm bound to wonder if there's more to it than what he told me?"

She smiled. "You think he's planning a fiddle?"

I felt a little foolish. "Stranger things have happened."

"Come *on*, Matt," she protested. "Would you have said that if he wasn't so dishy, and he didn't fancy me?"

Keeping my eye on the road ahead, I leaned across to kiss her on the cheek. "Probably not. I seem to have a built-in resistance to taking things on their face value ... I see intrigue where it doesn't exist."

"Oh, I'm sure there's plenty of that at Longlands. Nothing would surprise me about someone who installs a jacuzzi like that. I've been meaning to tell you ... you remember the three topless mermaids? Did you notice that the dark one ..."

The tangled thread of streets within the square mile of London's old boundaries is called the City. At the centre of the web is the Stock Exchange and the Bank of England, and such is the international importance of the concentration of financial institutions operating from this tiny area, that when people talk of "the City" they are usually referring to the activities conducted there more than the place itself. They spoke, for example, of Longstaff being in "the City", yet his offices were a few miles away in Portman Square, although such was his power and influence that more often than not the City came to him. The eight-storey red-brick premises owned by Allman & Spinks were imposing if slightly old-fashioned in comparison with the company's image of having one foot firmly planted in the 21st century. The marble-lined walls of the reception area on the ground floor had an unblemished shine about them, but the effect was dulled by the mottled beige colour scheme and the sombre maroons and dark blues of the huge Isfahan carpet which managed to retain its dignity despite some pretty threadbare patches near the middle. The same might have been said about the security man guarding the entrance to the lifts, who also looked as though he had seen better days.

However, the executive eighth floor had benefited from a comprehensive face-lift, and the pert blonde receptionist looked every bit as expensive as the fittings. Longstaff's office overlooked the green Portman Square. After the pretentiousness of Longlands it was surprisingly austere, as though Longstaff had Jekyll and Hyde personalities which he endeavoured to keep well apart. In fact, I was to discover there were no psychological overtones; simply that he was a creature of habit and could not countenance a change in the style of office he had occupied for fifteen years.

As I was announced he got up from a massive desk to greet me effusively, as though we had turned back the clock to the weekend party. I had expected a subtle change in his manner — for him to restore the slight distance between us, to make the relationship more formal – but the friendliness was reassuring. At least, he could not have had second thoughts over my relative inexperience. The force of his personality was so striking that it was not until we had shaken hands that I became aware of another man in the room, although I suppose it was not all that surprising since he was standing behind my line of vision which had been focussed on the advancing Longstaff.

Longstaff called his companion over to meet me and behind an automatic smile I studied him carefully. At first glance he seemed a personable chap of about my own age, although on closer inspection I suspected he was perhaps five or so years younger than me. His manner was relaxed and self-confident, although there was an erectness about his bearing, particularly his back and head, that made him look like an army physical-training instructor. The lightness of his tread, and firm handshake, confirmed that impression.

"Matthew Coll – David Morgan," announced Longstaff. "David is in charge of security for the group ..."

Morgan smiled, nothing false about the bonhomie; he seemed genuinely pleased to meet me. "I've heard some impressive things about you, Mr Coll."

"Oh ... ?" I was puzzled. On the strength of my Saturday-afternoon discussion with Longstaff there was little he could have discovered of interest. Then it dawned on me that I probably would not have been invited to Longlands unless Longstaff had been briefed in advance, and it would have been Morgan who had done the detective work. I bit back an indignant retort about abuse of privacy, realising how priggish it sounded, and forced a smile. They seemed so pleased with themselves; there was little point in rocking the boat.

"David and I were having our weekly meeting when you arrived, so I thought it would be a good idea if the two of you met," Longstaff said. "He has a very wide brief for the group. Looking after pension fund investments is an insignificant part of his work, but obviously he'll be involved when we start bringing valuable books into the building."

"As a matter of fact, I'd like to pick your brains, Mr Coll," Morgan cut in. "You probably know more about protecting books than I do ... "

I smiled. "The first thing is to check the small print on the insurance policy. You'll probably find you won't be covered unless the books were kept under lock and key 24 hours a day – which is really the *only* safe way to keep them, I suppose. The reason that there are so many thefts from libraries and other institutions is that by definition the books have to be left on display. It breaks my heart to think of rare books in a bank vault like bars of gold, but that's none of my business."

Longstaff chuckled. "I'm not such a heathen as you think I am. In fact, I've even discussed the matter with the group public relations manager to see if we could not get some mileage out of mounting an exhibition for the public. He suggested we might let one of the major libraries have the collection on some sort of permanent loan – which has a certain appeal."

"Good for the image ... "

"That was *his* idea, of course. I was thinking more specifically of saving in overheads."

"Overheads?" I echoed blankly, conscious that we were on different wavelengths.

"Insurance mainly. The budget I mentioned is one thing but we would have to insure the collection for at least half a million pounds, and the premiums on that sort of figure are not inconsiderable. It's a well-known fiddle to get the public institutions to fork out for the insurance. If it was two or three million I'd be more tempted; as it is the risk is too high for the saving – since we wouldn't even have control of the security arrangements. Some form of compromise is advisable ... that is, put them on display but here, where we can keep an eye on them."

"Display cabinets of some sort," interjected Morgan.

"Couldn't be better," I acknowledged. "Where do you keep the Turner?"

"In the board room – over the fireplace in full view, but bristling with alarms," Morgan replied. "Devices so sophisticated you even have to be careful what you *say* in front of it! For the books, we've set aside a conference room that is also used for receptions and big enough to house as many as a dozen large glass-topped cabinets. Problem is how best to safeguard them while keeping them accessible ... Different with the Turner; nobody is going to risk taking something of that magnitude."

"I've seen a few interesting installations. I'd be delighted to discuss them with you – or even introduce you to the libraries concerned."

He nodded appreciatively. "Your experience must be unique – books and army intelligence ... "

I did not like to be reminded of my spell in intelligence, which had not always been pleasant, and diverted him by asking if he had received his security training in the services.

"Hardly – unless you count the strongarm aspects. I was a PTI, and when I joined the company seven years ago it was as a uniformed guard. I was lucky enough to work my way up ... "

"No luck about it," Longstaff said, placing an arm around Morgan's shoulders and turning in the direction of the door. He paused with one hand on the door handle and turned his head. "The only thing that interests this company is ability," He turned back to Morgan. "I'll be in touch. Matt and I have one or two things to sort out right now .. will you excuse us?"

Smooth, I thought at the way the security man had been kicked out – so graciously.

Morgan and I exchanged waves and, when the door had closed behind him, Longstaff compensated for his summary dismissal, remarking: "Good chap, David. More important things on his plate than our books, so it pays to be nice to him."

"You seem to get on well enough ... ?"

"We respect each other. He has to be on his toes all the time. When I said 'more important' than books, I recognise that to you *nothing* could be more important, but being realistic you'd have to concede that one can at least insure against theft. Morgan's constant headache is the threat of industrial secrets being stolen. A company of our size is constantly working on programmes that are worth many millions of pounds. You can imagine what an attraction that must be to some people, and with three factories in the UK, apart from this place, and two regional sales offices, we are pretty vulnerable. Anyway I'm more concerned now with *buying* books, and not with the risk of losing them. What I want from you is a search programme that enables us to lay our hands on the sort of items we want. Presumably, all the *available* material, apart from auctions, is likely to be concentrated in a few dozen outlets?"

"Yes, I already get a few catalogues sent to the

shop, but I can get that stepped up and make a point – starting today, if you like – of visiting as many as I can of the more upmarket antiquarian shops. Apart from London I can reach practically everyone worthwhile by making a tour of the major university towns."

"I'll leave all that to you. Details don't worry me so much as the choice of books."

"Fine. We can draw up the guidelines together, but first I would like to know what sort of authority I'm going to have. I'd hardly expect to be given an open cheque-book, but perhaps we can agree on a limit?"

"Let's get the concept sorted out first ... for example, in the context of the size of our budget I can't see any point in buying anything under, say, £100. Theoretically, the ideal price would be in the region of £1000, which means we would be thinking in terms of about 300 volumes – which in security terms is manageable."

"I agree – if I am allowed to apply those guidelines flexibly. There might be some extremely good material available at £500; equally at £5000, even £50,000 – although, admittedly, at that figure, we would not get the same rate of growth."

"Flexibility, of course. That is where we need the expert advice. On the question of your authority, we will open an account which needs one signature for sums of under £250, for which you need not even consult me. For anything else on which we would need two signatures I would like you to send me the relevant details, and I will give you a decision within a couple of days."

I tried not to show my confusion. I had expected him to stipulate a second signature, but could not see the point of submitting written proposals when it was me – not him – who was supposed to be the expert. I tried to explain some of the problems that could arise. "There is the time factor. Something that pops up in a catalogue can't be reserved while we debate the issue. Couldn't we discuss that sort of case on the phone?"

He shook his head. "That's the way I prefer to work. Remember, we are not interested in *collecting* as such. If we miss out on an interesting title, we will not cry over spilt milk; we will simply wait for something else to console us."

I had no alternative but to accept Longstaff's conditions, which – providing he did not disappear on business trips for a few weeks at a time – I felt should not present any difficulties. My optimism would prove to be ill-founded.

By the time the meeting broke up just after midday I had gained a new respect for Longstaff. He may have been a playboy, but for someone who claimed to know nothing about rare books his ability to grasp essentials was remarkable, and I had the uneasy impression that if he bothered he was probably capable of dispensing with my services after a few months. It was probably something to do with his clinical approach – a quality which does not come easily to most booksellers. He would not be tempted to start browsing through a volume about to be catalogued, or distracted by something on the shelf so that it has to be taken down for further study at one's "leisure" – activities that would make any time-and-motion study expert clutch his hand to a fevered brow. Then he surprised me again with a suggestion that indicated that he was nevertheless human.

"Oh ... my wife is coming in for lunch today. I'd like you to meet her because you can do me a small favour. I don't spend as much time with her as I should, and I can't keep fobbing her off with expensive presents – bits of jewellery that she doesn't much like anyway. Having said you can forget about books under £100, that excluded anything really special that you feel I could buy as a present for her. In this case it doesn't matter a damn whether it's a good or bad investment – think only of aesthetic considerations."

"What *sort* of book would she like?"

He shrugged. "That's why I passed the buck to you. You had a quick look at her collection at Longlands. She's got a couple of thousand more at the London flat ... mainly paperbacks, although fairly serious literary material ... but you'll have a better idea from meeting her. I'm sure it is something you bibliophiles know instinctively. Let's just say something you'd like to give Laura as a present ..."

"Under £100?"

He thought for a few seconds. "Dammit. No. Use your discretion."

Ellen Longstaff was ten minutes late, but she was worth waiting for. It was immediately obvious why he had married her; she was the type of woman with whom most bachelors dream of settling down. Obviously intelligent, she was attractive but no knockout – but then who wants to be married to the beauty who turns every head in the room? It was bad enough being with someone as colourful as Laura but we were not married. It is a problem with which only the most laid-back of husbands can cope. Her clothes were smart and in excellent taste, but it was her naturalness that attracted me most. To me, intelligence and personality are prime requisites to sex appeal, and when our eyes met I knew instinctively she was my type, and why Longstaff had been prepared to sacrifice his freedom.

Ellen Longstaff had the composure and

sophistication that would enable her to mix well on any level and she complemented her husband perfectly. The other things I noticed about her at once were physical – her height (she was at least 5feet 9inches), and the soft ash-blond hair that framed an oval face like the aura of an angel ... perhaps I should have left it as "framing" her face, because there was certainly nothing angelic about it. Her voice was pleasantly husky and I liked her instinctively. If she had been at Longlands for the weekend there would have been an incentive to stay. And yet Longstaff still played the fool, by his own admission neglecting her. Studying her dispassionately I concede she lacked Laura's vividness, but then how could he mess about with topless models ...?

He had told her about me and it seemed her interest was genuine. "Pity I can't persuade Anthony to keep them at home," she said.

"We've been talking about security," Longstaff pointed out. "Much as I would like to oblige you I think the insurance company would put its foot down – Longlands is empty for most of the week ... " He turned to me to explain: "Our house in London is so convenient that we only go down to the country at weekends, or if one of us needs to entertain, so its pointless keeping a live-in staff. We get help locally as the need arises."

"I was thinking of London," she pointed out.

"There's not enough room to swing a cat. Where would you put them?"

She smiled. "We've got two spare bedrooms ... "

He raised his eyes to the ceiling and I interceded to prevent any friction in case she was serious. In any case, I was surprised by his remarks about Longlands. "Presumably you've got the usual security systems –

or else you would have been cleaned out by now."

"Enough for our needs, but there's nothing really valuable there."

The admission was another surprise and I admitted it.

"Think about it," he insisted. "Expensive *installations* such as the jacuzzi, the swimming-pool, the sauna ... and you wouldn't even believe what the squash court set me back ... but not the sort of thing that can be taken away. There's certainly no money, no jewellery and even the removable furniture and fittings are nothing special. I'm not foolhardy."

"And the alarm systems were chosen by David Morgan," added Ellen, "so we feel we can relax in the knowledge that the moment an unauthorized person steps into the house the local police will know about it."

"Then I support your case for having the new book collection at Longlands," I said. "Besides, it's nearer for me than London, and I can pop over from time to time to browse among the treasures we shall be acquiring."

"You don't need an excuse," she said, "You're welcome at any time anyway."

"That's true," Longstaff concurred.

His amiability intrigued me. We had nothing much in common and yet he was obviously keen to develop my relationship with his wife. I could only imagine that his philosophy was that the more she was occupied the less she would notice the complexity of his private life.

Four

While I could not afford to neglect the shop, the Allman & Spinks brief was exciting; not only because of the financial rewards, but for the opportunity it provided to handle fine books that, except in special cases, were outside the price range of my regular customers. Charlie Appleton, the retired bookseller who helped out when I was away for more than a day, took a fatherly interest in my welfare and was more than competent, so I knew I would not be missed for the amount of time involved.

In the event, I was able to embark on the programme whole-heartedly by devoting two or even three days a week to travelling and buying – without the customary apprehension, wondering whether one would ever get one's money back. In this case even the speculation had been removed; anything I fancied in the £250 category I was able to buy on the spot, while reserving everything else that needed Longstaff's confirmation. Admittedly the actual purchases were insignificant in relation to the far greater number of items that had to be reserved, but since that was surely only a formality, I derived tremendous aesthetic satisfaction from the experience.

The euphoria began to evaporate soon after I submitted the first list of thirty desirable acquisitions. I waited impatiently for a decision ... a day, two, three, until a week had elapsed – only to discover that Longstaff had accepted little more than half the list; the rest had been crossed off without comment. As far as I could see, there could be no objection to individual titles; nor was there any discernible pattern to the rejections, and I was so confused that I felt I had to insist on an explanation. But when I phoned, his secretary said he was in a meeting, and he apparently made no effort to return my call. When I caught up with him eventually, he claimed he was too busy to go over what he called "old ground."

Longstaff seemed surprised at my protestations, pointing out that there could be only one decision-maker. "It's not a committee matter," he said. "I thought I made it clear I had the final say … ?"

"I expected one or two disagreements – but not on this scale. Why employ an expert if you ignore his recommendations?"

"It's nothing personal. Your job is to locate the contents of our investment portfolio. We don't have to buy everything on offer, but at the end of the day they will all be your purchases. Just keep up the good work and we'll get there in the end … "

He had not given me a satisfactory answer so I persisted: "There were two or three items that stood out as exceptional value. There was a Book of Common Prayer that belonged to the diarist John Evelyn. It had his personal notes and marks in the margins. It's worth much more than the asking price as an association copy, apart from its antiquity. Then there was a Robert Boyle first edition … "

"Look Matt, I'm not a book-collector. Association copies mean nothing to me, and I don't have time for an inquest every time I turn down one of your suggestions."

He sounded irritable. I did not want to antagonise him, but there was a principle at stake. I laughed, hoping to ease the tension. "If you didn't turn them down in the first place there would be no need for an inquest. Admittedly, I mentioned the prayer-book because of my interest in John Evelyn, but I can be totally dispassionate about the Boyle. The last time a copy like this turned up at auction it fetched £13,000. We could have got this for £11,000, and in ten years' time it will be worth £20,000 ... it was a banker."

"That was also from the Evelyn library?"

I was pleasantly surprised that he had remembered, but endeavoured to correct his impression that I was biased, and retorted, "Anyone in the trade will tell you ..."

His snort of irritation pulled me up short. "If I may say so, Matt, you are behaving like a greedy child in a sweet-shop – grabbing at everything in sight. What's the hurry?"

I realised there was little to be gained in argument and backed down. Perhaps I should have stood my ground because unfortunately the pattern was repeated and when the same thing happened several times over the next few weeks I became increasingly angry. By his own admission Longstaff knew nothing about rare books yet he was arrogantly attempting to sit in judgement and blithely turning down at least half of the items that I had selected on their merits. On the last two occasions I was on the point of resigning the brief, but when I added up my commission and realised I had netted nearly £9,000 for the equivalent of eleven days' work, I overruled my pride and resisted the temptation.

Another consolation was the visit almost every week to the Allman & Spinks headquarters to watch the collection growing. After consultation with me and a firm of specialists, David Morgan had purchased glass display units so that the highlights of our collection could be shown off to their best advantage – usually opened to show the title page or a special feature such as the illustrations or bindings and craftsmanship. The explanatory notes I had provided on the books and their history had been artistically embellished by a professional calligrapher, and the effect was an eye-stopper even to the uninitiated.

Some of the purchases seemed to be slow in reaching the display, but that was hardly my concern, and in all other respects I was made to feel a valued member of the team. I was even presented with a pass that enabled me to move about the building freely, and keys to the cabinets – a privilege, since only Longstaff and Morgan had the others. It was as though I was the curator of an important library than an itinerant bookseller, and this to some extent offset the annoyance of not being able to insist on my first choices.

So the financial and aesthetic rewards served to justify my decision not to resign when I read in a brief report in the morning newspapers of Longstaff's mysterious disappearance. Although it merited only a single-column headline it was important enough for the front page of my morning newspaper. The print seemed to stand out on the page. I had no affection for the man and I must admit that my immediate reaction was a combination of curiosity and anxiety – prompted by the purely selfish realisation that a lucrative source of income was now in jeopardy. The coverage was short, presumably because of the implication that there was nothing sinister in his disappearance. I read it over and over again:

'Police are investigating the disappearance of Anthony Longstaff, financial director of Allman &

Spinks, the pharmaceuticals empire. Mr Longstaff failed to arrive for a business meeting in Southampton yesterday. Enquiries revealed that Mr Longstaff had reserved accommodation at a Lymington hotel but did not sign the register, although his car was found in the hotel car park. Clothing belonging to the financier was found on a private beach at Lepe, a few miles away. Foul play is not suspected.'

Reading between the lines, one would either assume that Longstaff had gone for a swim and accidentally drowned, or that he had committed suicide. Either assumption was hard to swallow, although I was forced to remind myself that I scarcely knew Longstaff the man, as opposed to the business machine, and that even my suspicious mind had no grounds for questioning the apparent facts. My sense of logic wriggled. What *facts*? The report was sparse yet within the first couple of lines Longstaff had been described incorrectly as the company's financial director; what else did they have wrong?

Although I knew that Longstaff's business projects would have the automatic support of the Board, and that existing projects would probably be completed by one of his assistants, or by a new supremo brought in, and that I would simply have to mark time for the present, I felt an obligation to phone David Morgan and double-check with him. Morgan sounded upset, which was hardly surprising since I knew he respected Longstaff, but he refused to concede that the missing man was dead. However, it soon transpired that he knew nothing but the bare facts and was as bewildered as everyone, including Ellen Longstaff.

What I did not tell him at this stage was that, three

days before, I had finally succeeded in fulfilling the personal commission in which Longstaff had entrusted me – to find a book for his wife. His disappearance put me in a difficult position because although the purchase had been authorised, I could hardly send it in the usual manner to Allman & Spinks with an invoice; nor could I ask Ellen Longstaff for the money. The book was the 5th edition of 1641 of Beaumont and Fletcher's *The Maid's Tragedie*. It had a delightfully theatrical woodcut illustration on the title-page of Aminter running his sword through Aspatia. It was attractive enough to add to my own stock for future resale, but I felt a moral obligation to hand it over to Ellen, particularly as it was probably the last gift she would ever receive from her husband – even if it meant footing the bill myself. I decided that would be my course of action. I had earned enough from Longstaff's brief, so this would be a mark of my gratitude. The only remaining problem was *when* to give it to her; I could not intrude on her grief, at least not for another few days.

Meanwhile, I was puzzled over what might have happened to Longstaff and was not prepared to be as passive as Morgan.

I toyed with the idea of ringing George Kester, the Daily Chronicle columnist with whom I had once been on friendly terms, but decided that it was probably premature. It would take more than a day for journalists to get at the facts behind the initial police statement, which was so typically vague. Meanwhile the police were my best bet, and since the only evidence – the clothing – had been found a stone's throw away on the Hampshire/Dorset borders, my friend Detective Inspector Murdoch of Ardley CID might have an ear to the ground.

Murdoch was a striking figure who might have passed for a 19th-century country squire, or a character from a Thomas Hardy novel, out of touch with modern society, especially criminals. In fact, it was an image he cultivated. The ginger mutton-chop sideburns and shaggy eyebrows that overhung his blue eyes – giving him a sheepdog look – seemed to be part of the disguise that encouraged people to underestimate him. But not only was Murdoch as sharp as any of his counterparts at Scotland Yard, he had a terrier-like quality that made me realise from the start of our relationship that he was not the sort of man to fall out with. He was also physically strong, despite a now permanent stiffness in his lower back that indicated an arthritic condition, although he was only in his early forties.

Our friendship had come under strain from time to time when my efforts to uphold the law had intruded on police territory (not to say, ridden roughshod over it) but we had an understanding. Murdoch was capable of turning a blind eye so long as I did not overstep the mark on his "patch".

Since one of Murdoch's complaints was that he never saw me unless I was in trouble, he could hardly grumble now if I rang him to enquire after his health ... and, in the course of friendly chat, casually mention the mystery that had landed in the lap of his colleagues along the coast ... ?

But my opening gambit was brushed aside with mock contempt. "You *want* something, as usual, so don't waste my time with all that bullshit. Ten to one you're involved with this financier Longstaff ..."

"How did you know?" I said, as mildly as I could, trying not to let him guess he had taken the wind out of my sails.

"Nothing happens in *Ardley* these days; even our phantom 'flasher' seems to have died of boredom, and you wouldn't be asking me about crime in London. Sorry I can't help you – but my patch doesn't extend to Southampton ... "

"Don't tell me you don't know the officer in charge. He's probably one of your fishing cronies ... "

"What is he to you?"

"Nothing. I don't care *who* you go fishing with ... "

"*Longstaff*, I mean. Why are you interested in him?"

I hesitated and decided there was nothing wrong with the truth. "Idle curiosity really – but he also happens to be a customer ... "

There was a note of triumph in Murdoch's grunt of acknowledgment. "I thought so! Why didn't you come straight to the point? What is there to hide?"

I sniggered. "Intimidation won't get you anywhere. If you had asked me nicely I would have told you. How did you guess, anyway?"

"I do see other papers apart from *Fishing News* and *Farmers Weekly*. Haven't I read about him before in the context of pension funds? Isn't he supposed to the doyen of investment analysts?"

I said I was more interested in how he had linked Longstaff with me than discussing the City, and he laughed at my bewilderment. "I hadn't given it a thought – until you rang. I knew his firm had bought the Turner, and paintings as an investment are not so far removed from books – so your enquiry was too much of a coincidence."

I gave him an account of my dealings with Longstaff, pointing out that they were supposed to be secret to prevent rival pension funds from stealing a march on us. Murdoch was intrigued. He had little more information than me, but promised to make enquiries and phone me back, although when he returned my call within the hour he was not as forthcoming as I had expected.

"Inspector Hopwood is not one of my fishing cronies so I had to declare your interest – and the upshot is that he wants me to get a statement."

"I've no objection. What's your moan?"

He sighed. "Despite what I said about the flasher retiring, I have got enough on my plate without doing Hopwood's legwork too. Besides, I know from bitter experience that by the time you've censored the information you deign to give us, it will be worse than useless ..."

The cynicism was tongue-in-cheek, but I had to play him along. "That's Hopwood's problem – not yours. I wouldn't deny it – *if* I had a vested interest. On this occasion I haven't, apart from an unpleasant feeling I'm going to miss Mr Longstaff financially. Presumably your colleagues think there might be more to it than meets the eye?"

"Let's say they're keeping an open mind. Apparently Longstaff was pretty fit, and a good swimmer. It is just possible he decided to stroll down to the beach for a swim before turning in ..."

"Why walk a couple of miles when he could take the car?"

"Seems he was a fitness fanatic. Like a lot of men his age, he didn't like the idea of growing old."

"What about the tide?"

"Assuming he took his dip late evening, it would have been going out, which could have added another dimension ... and caused a heart attack. It's equally possible that he set out to drown himself. Ideal time; no-one about. No suicide note – at least nothing we've found yet – but it's not uncommon with businessmen of his stature. With all the projects he was balancing in the air at the same time the strain must have been enormous ... "

"What was he doing in this neck of the woods?"

"Buying a few hundred acres of land. Apparently some enormous deal with the Forestry Commission ... timber as a long-term investment ... several millions of pounds involved."

I had a kaleidoscopic mental picture of Longstaff "wheeling and dealing" and marvelled at the man's grasp of such a variety of commercial disciplines. Yet that had been his life, and it was impossible to imagine him bowing to pressure, or allowing it to build up until it exploded. "What other possibilities are there?" I enquired cautiously.

"You would have to ask Hopwood, not me. I told you they're keeping an open mind."

"It's been done before, of course ... "

"What has?"

"Clothes on the beach. There was a television comedy series about a man who was so fed up with life that he decided to disappear – in the same way."

"Sounds hilarious."

"It was, as it happens. But you know that truth is stranger than fiction. What about the case of the former Postmaster General who did much the same thing – only that was serious ... ? Went to the United States on business and also left his hotel to go for a swim ... "

" ... and turned up in Australia? Is that what you think Longstaff has done?"

I thought about it for a few seconds. "It makes more sense than suicide. But if he was running away there would have to be a damn good reason. I certainly can't think of one. As far as I could see Longstaff was living it up anyway – having his cake and eating it. What more could he want?"

Murdoch promised to pop into the shop later to take a formal statement, and when I put the phone down I was perplexed. Longstaff was a financial genius. Had he pulled off a gigantic confidence trick? On reflection, starting a new life somewhere with a few million pounds stashed away might have its attractions to a hedonist like him ... never again having to go through the motions of respectability ... spending the rest of his days in the pursuit of pleasure. For a man of his intellect, perhaps even the planning and carrying out of the perfect crime might be incentive enough.

Now was the time to call George Kester. It was background I was after, not news. I did not know enough about the City to speculate about possible fraud. I needed an expert and George would introduce me to his City editor. I was scheduled to make one of my regular trips to London in a couple of days time and fortunately he was able to arrange an appointment for me with Richard Schlessinger for that morning. I decided I would take the gift for Ellen Longstaff and drop it round to her later, providing Morgan said that she was bearing up well enough under the strain.

I knew a number of the Chronicle reporters, but had not met Schlessinger. He had joined the paper six months before from a rival journal in a blaze of publicity that claimed him to be the best informed journalist in the City. Kester had obviously implied that while I merely wanted to pick his brains, I could be relied upon to return the compliment if there was a story to be had at the end of the line, and he was suitably attentive.

Schlessinger, a dapper man in his forties, wore his mousy-coloured hair very short, almost in a crop as though trying to conceal the onset of baldness, and watery blue eyes squinted short-sightedly at me behind thick, rimless spectacles. He was not much to look at, but he was certainly no fool. There was no way I could prevent him from guessing whom my enquiries were about, so I put my cards on the table and prayed that he adhered to the journalistic code and would keep a confidence. Telling him that I doubted whether Longstaff had accidentally drowned, or committed suicide, I postulated my theory that he might have been engaged in a fraud of some magnitude.

He grimaced even before I had completed my speculation. "I didn't hear that, Mr Coll, and I urge you to be careful where you make such highly libellous statements. I'm not suggesting that the City is populated by angels, but in relation to the vast sums of money changing hands all the time, the incidence of fraud is *very* small. People who run pension funds are more accountable for their investments than most speculators, and the only information I have about Longstaff is that he was a boy genius who actually made good – one of the few who wasn't consumed by the brightness and intensity of his own flame."

I objected to his manner but reminded myself that I would get nowhere without his help. "I accept all that, and I'll take your advice. Forget individuals. Can we just talk theory?"

He relaxed instantly and when he smiled the lines disappeared and he suddenly looked like a studious schoolboy. "Why not? Fire away."

I phrased the question carefully. "Let's pretend you've given up journalism to try your hand at investment. You've done well for a while and you're in a position of some authority; at least, in terms of financial muscle …"

"I'm running a pension fund … " he interjected solemnly.

I nodded. "As I said, you are doing well – *so* well that no-one would notice if you were to cream off some of that excess profit for yourself … "

"Why would I do that? We've just heard I've done very well for myself!"

I looked at him sharply and then realised he was merely taking his part seriously, establishing the role like a method actor. "Success is always relative. Whatever you've earned, you've been living above your means. Now you're heavily in debt and because of your reputation you can't even approach the bank for a loan. The only thing you can rely on is your brain …"

Schlessinger's eyes were closed and he was racking his brain for a solution to his problem. He began to think aloud, as though in a trance. "Whom do I know that I could trust? I really need a front man who need not even know what's going on … " He stopped and I was quite convinced he was trying to think of one of his own friends.

He was silent for more than a minute and becoming impatient I interrupted his train of thought. "Assuming Mr X had such a friend, what are the options open to him?"

Schlessinger opened his eyes reluctantly and dropped the façade to become more businesslike. "How much do you know about the stock market?" he demanded.

"Nothing."

"Then, with all due respect, most of the possibilities

that spring to mind would be over your head." He shrugged, and then obviously thought better of his negative attitude. "There *are* a couple of ploys which are basically very simple and therefore easy to follow ... " He looked at me expectantly and I nodded. "Well, if one had what you called 'muscle' — really big money – it can be used to push up the price of shares. It requires a fine degree of subtlety, but assuming it was done with the help of a leg-man it should be possible to make a quick killing."

"How would one check it out if you had suspicions?"

"If Mr X was not too greedy it would be next to impossible."

"What would you call a modest operation? A few thousand pounds?"

Schlessinger nodded. "No-one would look too closely at that sort of gain, providing it didn't happen often. It's less hassle, of course, not to play the market at all – simply take cut-backs ... "

"But that would make Mr X rather vulnerable, surely?"

"I wasn't talking about anything underhand. A lot of people get their income from what you might call 'finder's fees', that is being able to set up a substantial loan and getting an agreed commission ... "

"How big could a finder's fee be?"

He shrugged. "I know someone who recently got three quarters of one per cent on £1 million ... and that is not uncommon."

I did a rapid calculation. "Sounds like easy money, but why would anyone need the services of an intermediary?" I recalled Longstaff's remarks on the risk factor and added, "If the borrower is so desperate presumably he's already hawked his prospectus around without any luck, so there is more an element of risk involved. Our Mr X surely wouldn't take that sort of chance just for a few thousand quid on the side."

He laughed. "Borrowing a million is not like asking your friendly bank manager for an overdraft, even though it might be just as simple most of the time. The fact that half a dozen people turn you down means nothing – probably just illustrates their lack of vision. It's not just what you can show on the balance sheets, believe me ..." He began to elaborate and I smiled to show my interest, but closed my mind to the lecture. I realised I was learning nothing. How Longstaff might have earned money on the side was not the point. *Had* he, was what mattered, and the easier line of enquiry would be to establish *why* he might have resorted to swindle.

Five

It had not occurred to me that Ellen Longstaff was anything but a woman of leisure who, between entertaining her husband's associates, would wind down at the beauty salon and recharge her batteries from a charge account at Harrods. This preconceived notion meant that when I rang their Kensington home from the Chronicle offices, it was disconcerting to discover that "Madam" could be found "at work". I was given another number which, it transpired, was a lively fringe theatre company, the "Garden Stage", located in one of the turnings off the Earls Court Road. As I was to learn, Mrs Longstaff was general manager, head cook and bottle-washer.

Ellen answered the phone herself, business-like but friendly; a tone that warmed by several degrees when I identified myself. I don't suppose I had expected her to sound distraught, but the cheerfulness was not easy to reconcile with the image one inevitably had of a woman whose husband had disappeared only a few days before. Instinctively I wondered whether her interest in the theatre extended to acting – in which case it was an impressive performance. Perhaps if the marriage itself was an act she had no reason to be upset, or perhaps she was simply not worried because she knew there was no cause – that all the time Longstaff was somewhere alive and well.

I explained that I had a book for her, without elaborating, and offered to bring it round to the theatre, but she had a hectic day ahead and asked, if it was convenient to me, if I could deliver it to the house later. I had planned to pop in to the Allman & Spinks offices to see David Morgan and then catch an early-evening train back to Dorset, but I had no hesitation in postponing my return. I even toyed with the idea of inviting her to have dinner with me, but decided that might be presumptuous – perhaps even in bad taste in the circumstances, and agreed to call on her at seven.

After a pub lunch with George Kester, who as a newsman was far more interested in the disappearance of Anthony Longstaff than Schlessinger had been, I took a taxi from Fleet Street to Portman Square. The traffic was horrendous and I congratulated myself for not bringing the car to London; indeed for managing to stay away from the capital as much as I did. I had Ellen's book in my briefcase and, because of the possible confusion over its ownership, I decided to deposit the case at reception. I also left a message for Morgan that I could be found in the conference room where the book collection, still growing, was housed.

The company's conference facility was basically one 50-feet-x-30-feet room, which could be converted into separate units by folding partition doors in the middle. In practice, even with a handful of people, the doors usually remained open, and the open space with its high ceiling could have passed for a ball-room; the highly polished parquet floor doing nothing to dispel that impression. The room was situated near the centre of the building on the eighth floor, which meant that there were no windows, but its size prevented any sense of claustrophobia; the concealed lighting was effective and the air-conditioning flexible enough to cope with a crowd, or a single person.

When not in use it was sparsely furnished with small tables and chairs, but eight display cabinets were now a permanent addition, although as yet only four contained books. They stood in a line almost down the full length of the room, compelling attention. Whether it was their size – they were three feet high x two feet – or the classic simplicity of their design, they had an air of majesty. Laid out on two levels, each separately lit, the cabinets could house between eight-twelve books, depending on their size. Behind them, along a twenty-foot expanse between two doors, bookshelves had been erected, protected by sliding glass panels. This area was reserved for those volumes that did not merit individual display, although even this section was locked and could not be opened without the authority of Longstaff, Morgan or myself.

It was the first time I had been in the room since Longstaff had disappeared, and it seemed almost eerie that nothing had changed, as though I had expected the collection to vanish along with the man who had been responsible for their assembly. Everything seemed in order and there was little point in staying, but I hesitated over leaving so quickly in case Morgan was on his way to see me. The thin rows of books on the wall facing me – as yet no more than one hundred – looked rather forlorn, almost lost within that vast expanse of shelving, and I walked over, as though to reassure them that they all merited attention; that, it was to be hoped, they were merely the vanguard of a great collection.

Unlocking the glass panel I slid it aside to expose the books, each one a delight in itself, and idly selected the volume in line with my right arm. It was not until I had the book in my hand that I realised that the title was in German. It was the first edition of Sigmund Freud's *Die Traumentung*, nothing much to look at but because of its significance worth every penny of the £1200 I had paid for it. However, since my German is abysmal there was little point in dipping into the text and I was about to return it, unopened, to the shelf when I changed my mind. To this day I cannot say *why* I looked at the title-page, other than that it was an instinctive gesture – the way one looks at one's watch without really registering the time. I was about to close the covers again when an alarm-bell in my subconscious was activated and I turned back to the title-page. Published Berlin 1928? The volume I had bought was published in Leipzig in 1900 – in other words the *original* edition! It was one of the books that had been reserved by a dealer in Edinburgh while awaiting Longstaff's decision, and it looked as though he had sent the wrong edition in error. I tried to picture the copy I had reserved, but my memory was hazy; I had seen several hundred books in my travels over the past couple of months and although I seemed to recall the colour of the cloth binding had been the same, it had surely not been as fine as this ... I was irritated at the carelessness of the bookseller concerned and wondered if he still had the first edition I had intended to order.

Instead of replacing the book, I put it on top of one of the display cabinets, intending to draw it to Morgan's attention, or to that of one of Longstaff's assistants. My eyes returned to the bookshelves. Now, several of the bindings seemed unfamiliar and I was surprised that having cost so much money they had not impressed themselves on my memory more clearly. I selected another, expecting the title-page to bring the initial reaction flooding back and had another shock – this was not one of my purchases either; at least, it was the same title but not the same copy. With sinking heart, I wondered how many books had been replaced by inferior copies. It was too much of a coincidence that two reputable booksellers had sent the wrong books in error, even more than it had been done deliberately. And if someone had tampered with the books on the shelves, then perhaps the display cabinets would also provide some shocks. My gaze flitted, panic-stricken, over the regimented spines facing me, not daring to risk disappointment by further checks, but then I saw an old volume too shabby to ignore and took it down to find it *was* a first edition but almost disbound and with most of the plates loose; the copy I had bought had been fine and the difference in value was probably more than £1500.

I decided to find Morgan, or someone in whom I could confide. Preoccupied as I was, I sensed that someone had come into the room ... nothing that I actually heard, more an intuition. *Did Morgan have a juvenile sense of humour*? I looked round, intending to shake him by my coolness.

It was me who was shaken. The close proximity of an unexpected face further distorted by a stocking mask made my stomach turn over. Within the space of that split second I did my best to recognise the face, but it was impossible. All I could be sure of was that it was a man about my own height and build and that he was dressed in blue denim overalls like a workman ... a service engineer. He was wearing black leather gloves and I looked for other distinguishing features ... a wrist-watch perhaps ... but there was nothing. Even as these facts were processed and fed into the print-out in my mind, I was swaying my head to one side to avoid the spanner aimed at my head. Conscious of the man's right hand in a scything arc from right to left, I moved in the opposite direction to sweep inside it. It was the correct action to take ... if only I had another split second to spare; as it was, the impact of metal on bone – the left side of my temple – was a glancing one, but enough to scramble my senses.

I could still think clearly; in fact, I distinctly remember feeling how lucky I was that the blow had been on the hardest part of my head – a few inches behind and I might have suffered serious injury – yet my limbs were incapable of obeying the order to fight back. It was as though I was trying to support an enormous weight, or that an invisible ceiling was bearing down on me. I sank to my knees, seeking a momentary respite so that I could bring my limbs under control but it was beyond me. I was conscious of being pushed to the floor and my attacker rummaging through my trouser pockets for the keys to the display cabinets. I could do nothing as he moved over to the nearest cabinet and unlocked the door.

I realise in retrospect that although I had assumed that my head was clear and that it was my body that had let me down, it was really the other way about. If I had been in full possession of my faculties, I would have done nothing ... simply lain on the floor recovering my wits and strength while he stripped the cabinets – there would have been ample time – but instead I reacted instinctively with no more guile than an animal protecting its territory. I barely had enough strength to lift myself on to all fours – in fact, I was reasonably sure I could not get up properly – but he had his back to me so I was able to crawl forward and clutch at his leg in a clumsy imitation of a rugby tackle. I had no strength, but I clung to his thigh like a limpet, and 175 lbs does provide a makeshift anchor. Unable to pull free, he kicked me in the stomach and side with his free leg, but I was barely conscious of the pain.

However, when he retrieved the spanner from his pocket and raised it to strike me again I knew it was foolhardy not to let go. In the struggle we had switched positions and, aware of the heavy display case behind me offering some measure of support, I pulled myself up on his overalls while he tried to force me back to get some leverage for the spanner. I grabbed for his right wrist – momentarily disconcerted by its surprising smoothness – but it was only a token effort and I did not have the strength to retain my grip. He was trying to push me away and clutching at straws I tried to use his momentum by suddenly letting go, and allowing his push to carry me backwards – against the glass cabinet. It was heavy enough to withstand the ordinary force of someone overbalancing against it, but before impact I raised my forearms in a judo break-fall position and brought them down hard on the glass – followed by the full weight of my body. To my chagrin the glass did not immediately shatter but the cabinet did lose its equilibrium and slowly began to tip over, and I felt myself propelled backwards with it. Hitting the ground it seemed to explode and simultaneously the pain returned, although this time it was everywhere.

The sensation of losing consciousness was like falling down a black hole, except that I was floating down quite comfortably and the sense of apprehension was alleviated by the sound of an ambulance following. The bell was painfully strident, more like an alarm, yet it was strangely reassuring, meaning that help was close at hand. I smiled as it carried me off.

When I awoke in Middlesex Hospital it was as though I had enjoyed a long relaxing sleep. Although I did not remember arriving, the only thing that surprised me about the surroundings was that I was in a private room, and there was already a vase of fresh flowers on the bedside cabinet. I sat up to ring for a nurse and a sharp pain in my head cut the effort short halfway. I remembered the cause of my discomfort and gingerly lifted a hand to my forehead. I could feel a massive swelling and bruising but no dressing, indicating that stitches had not been required, but the movement caused me to notice the heavy bandage on my left forearm. I recalled the smashed glass and looked at my other arm, instantly relieved to find no bandage, only three strips of lightweight plaster, no doubt concealing a few superficial scratches. Assured that nothing was broken I raised myself again, closing my eyes against the pain, and rang the communications bell.

The attractive staff nurse who breezed in on cue was

annoyingly cheerful. "Feeling better, are we?"

"Yes," I lied. "When can I go?"

Her only answer was to thrust a thermometer into my mouth, and having shut me up she proceeded to take my pulse. As I tried to register my disgust she smiled brightly which made her a little less inhuman. She told me that in cases where consciousness had been lost there was the possibility of concussion so I would have to stay in hospital overnight. "The doctor is only playing safe," she insisted. "The X-rays are fine."

I groaned mentally at the prospect of wasting a night in hospital, but resisted the impulse to complain; it was nothing to do with her. "If I was unconscious, whose decision was it to put me in here? If I've got to foot the bill, I'd prefer a hotel – it's cheaper ..."

She moved closer purposefully, fluffed up my pillows and smoothed the bedclothes. "You don't get *this* sort of personal service in a hotel," she said with a mischievous wink and, although I knew it was only an act, I was amused. "Anyway, you're not paying," she added. "It was the gentleman outside. I'll send him in ..."

"Wait a minute," I interjected. "What about my cuts and bruises. Am I going to live?"

"Just about ... " she replied poker-faced. "Twelve stitches in the left arm ... quite nasty that cut, three or four apiece in the other and nothing on your back. It looks a mess but they are just scratches. You seem to have been quite lucky."

It was David Morgan who replaced her and after the phoney cheerfulness his miserable expression was almost a consolation. At least it was natural. Morgan looked genuinely concerned at my battered appearance – apparently my left eye was beginning to blacken – and when I thanked him for the private room he shrugged it off with a string of platitudes. I made a meal of it, using the small talk as a smoke-screen while I tried to decide on my attitude. I had found evidence of fraud. *Someone* was responsible; someone who knew what Longstaff (through me) was trying to achieve. I could not forget that only three of us had keys, yet surely Morgan must have realised that he would automatically come under suspicion. *Are you as innocent as you appear*?

During my fight with the thief I had been at a disadvantage from start to finish, so frustratingly there had been no opportunity to tear off the mask. The overalls could have been misleading, but he had seemed roughly the same build as me – and therefore the same as Morgan – yet he had not been particularly agile, whereas I had the impression Morgan would move like a cat if the occasion arose. On reflection, I was reasonably sure that my assailant was not Morgan, but there were other disquieting factors. Only Morgan knew I was in the building, that is, apart from the receptionist – so he could have arranged the attack, even if it was not him. Furthermore, some of the books had been replaced at some time during the past few weeks and that would almost certainly have to be an inside job.

He shook his head when I asked if the intruder had been caught. "The alarm attracted attention, of course, but he had vanished by the time the first persons arrived. I was there soon afterwards but came here with you in the ambulance. When I'd got you settled, I went back to find out what the hell had happened, and it seems the only person not accounted for was a service engineer from the alarm company; at least, that is who they assumed he was – from his pass. We checked with the firm, and of course they didn't send anyone today."

"Unfortunately he was wearing a stocking mask ..."

"He would have taken that off straight-way, but the overalls would have given him a degree of anonymity. He would have gone down the back stairs and then used any permutation of exits, not that anyone would necessarily have given him a second glance."

"Did he get away with anything?"

"He took off in a panic. I don't think so, but I couldn't be sure."

"That's something," I conceded. "Any ideas?"

"If you're feeling up to it, perhaps we can compare notes. I've got all the theory, the sort of knowledge that impresses the board, but I'm short on practical experience. It's more your cup of tea."

His apparent trust in me was touching. I smiled. "A crack on the head makes everyone equal ... "

"What I meant was: what was your gut reaction? Would you say he was a pro?"

I shrugged and the movement of my diaphragm reminded me of the bruising around my stomach and side. I would never have admitted it but I was secretly relieved at being forced to stay in bed; and yet, painful as those kicks had been, they were totally ineffective at the time. "There are professionals and professionals," I hedged. "He wasn't very good, and he panicked."

"It takes a lot of nerve to hang about with an alarm-bell sounding off right in your ear."

"If he bluffed his way in, he could have done the same again. All he had to do was to look scared, point in the opposite direction and yell: 'he went *that* way'. No-one would have argued ... they would have stood around like sheep waiting for someone to take charge.

If *I* had gone in to steal something, I wouldn't have gone without it – especially after going to all that trouble ... "

"You think it was carefully planned ... that he was waiting for you?"

"*Someone* knew that only three of us had keys – two of us, in fact, now that Tony Longstaff has vanished. That person had the option of going for you – or for me. We have to ask ourselves why he chose me? Especially as I only come here once a week at most ... "

"Although always on the same day."

"And who knows that?"

Morgan pulled a face. "Only me. I can't think of anyone else, apart from Jessie, the receptionist, or a shrewd guess on the part of one of my uniformed men. I'm also the only one who knew about the keys ... "

I smiled. "The thought had occurred to me ... "

He did not share the joke. "It wasn't me, Mr Coll. Why would I complicate things? I could have got the books at any time of the day or night, without resorting to violence ... "

"That occurred to me too," I acknowledged. I conceded that I was reasonably sure that he had not been my attacker, but while I talked I was weighing up the pros and cons of mentioning my discovery of the switch in books and the fraud it probably represented. I doubted whether Morgan knew enough about rare books to be working that sort of fiddle, but more to the point it would be more difficult to prove. I decided there was nothing to lose by telling him, so that I could at least gauge his reactions.

He was visibly shattered. I watched closely for any indication that he was putting on an act. I am not easily fooled, and Morgan was not only upset, but embarrassed that the security system he had devised at great expense had been almost useless. I explained the differences in value between original editions and reprints, between fine copies and those bearing signs of wear and tear. "I don't know how many replacements you'll find. I found three in the only three that I examined, which is bloody ominous, but you'll have to go through my checklist as a matter of priority. *Any* divergence from what I've included on the stocklist – even if they look the same to you – must be treated with suspicion ... it's a frightening proposition ... "

"You mean the collection might be valueless?"

"Not entirely valueless, but worth considerably less than its face value. We may have nipped it in the bud, but if Longstaff had not disappeared and so stopped us buying, in theory at the end of the project we might have had a £300,000 investment worth next to nothing ..."

Morgan rubbed his chin reflectively. He seemed about to say something but changed his mind and stood up. "I'll be getting back to the office," he announced.

I knew the checklist would take him hours. "If you can find the doctor to let me out, I'll come with you – it will save a lot of time."

"Thanks, but I can manage, and it's my responsibility. In any case, I forgot to tell you, your suit is pretty well ruined. The firm will pay for a new one since it was damaged in what we might call the line of duty. In the morning I'll bring you something from my wardrobe – we're more or less the same size."

The thought of him going back to the office reminded me that my briefcase was still in reception, and in it the book for Ellen. I told him about it and, as I hoped, he dutifully took the bait.

"I'll phone her," he promised, "and bring your case back in the morning with the spare clothes."

"The case isn't so urgent; I don't use it very much – but I won't be in town again until next week so perhaps you could arrange for a messenger to deliver the book."

"No need. I'll drop it in this evening on my way home."

I thanked him, embarrassed at passing the buck. By the time he had finished going through my checklist, he'd be lucky to get to her house by midnight. Idly I wondered where he lived, but when he had left the room I suddenly stopped worrying about his problems and started feeling sorry for myself. I had been attached to my old grey tweed suit. Laura complained that it was shapeless, but I felt comfortable in it. Old clothes are like friends; we might take them for granted but we miss them when they've gone. I did not want a new suit with or without the compliments of Allman & Spinks; nor did I relish the prospect of wearing one of Morgan's immaculate three-piece business suits. It might look all right on him, but it was hardly me. Even Laura would concede that.

Laura! My conscience nagged at me. I had been too preoccupied with the missing Longstaff to tell her I would be in London. We would normally have spent the evening together, but much as I would have enjoyed her fussing over me now, I was too embarrassed to ring so late, more or less admitting it was an afterthought. I was under no illusion over my tendency to take her for granted, but it was not something I would consciously do.

Six

There had been no news of Longstaff for ten days. I understood from Inspector Murdoch that the police were leaning towards the theory that he was alive and had planned to disappear. Interpol and law-enforcement agencies farther afield had been alerted, but the police admitted that the prospects of finding him were slim; evidence of the past had shown that it was not difficult for someone of intelligence – especially a man with money and resources – to vanish without trace.

Officials of Scotland Yard's fraud squad had sniffed around in the early stages, but there were no fundamental grounds for suspicion. Allman & Spinks was a powerful organisation; when they refused to allow the Pension Fund books to be examined, pompously maintaining that they were audited by one of the country's most distinguished firm of accountants, the enquiry did not even get off the ground. When it came to Longstaff's personal finances, the police were able to exert their own authority, but again drew a blank. What I had imagined to be an extravagant lifestyle was in fact limited to certain areas of interest. He had only one car, and did not own a yacht or a helicopter, as did some of his associates, so there was little to indicate that he was living beyond his means.

I reconciled myself to a long delay, whatever happened. His colleagues were shrewd men but hardly entrepreneurs, and while there had never been any reason to question his judgement they would wait until the last possible moment before committing themselves to any course of action over the projects that awaited completion.

After my release from hospital I had a warm note from Ellen Longstaff thanking me for being the instrument of her husband's generosity. I remember wincing at the reminder of how much his generosity had cost me, but I had been hoist on my own petard so there was little point on brooding over the matter. But a week later she telephoned to ask if we could meet when I was next in London.

This time I was invited to dinner. I was ridiculously pleased, wondering if I would be the only guest, until a pang of conscience prompted me to phone Laura to see if I might call on her later that evening. It seemed like fate because she too had a date – she was being taken to the theatre – but wanted me to call at the flat later (to let myself in if she had not yet returned) provided I did not mind sharing coffee with the man who would have been her companion for the evening. If I was honest with myself I did mind, but my conscience was a stern taskmaster and would make me grin and bear it. However, I consoled myself with the picture of my rival departing after coffee – with me, having appeared from nowhere, now in residence.

The trip to London was doubly convenient because I had to have my stitches removed and, apart from a little tenderness in my left arm, which still required a small dressing, I was given a clean bill of health.

The Longstaff home off Kensington High Street was one of those red-brick town houses on four floors, in a terrace. From the front they looked cramped, but only because it was not possible to see how far back they stretched. The door was opened by a manservant in a fawn jacket, but Ellen was on the stairs to the first-floor living-quarters. She had chosen her spot well, her full-length bottle-green velvet housecoat, slit at the front to just over the knees, stood out richly against the lush brown stair-carpet and white banisters. She looked every bit the elegant hostess that one admires in a TV After Eight chocolates commercial.

Taking my hand she said how nice it was of me to come at such short notice, as though my social diary was committed months ahead. It may have been a common enough platitude, but it sounded as though she meant every word. *Sincere* is the word I should have used, but then such is my cynicism that I believe that sincerity should be demonstrated, but not heard – and it had the opposite effect to the one she probably intended. I admired sophistication in a woman, but her coolness reminded me of her husband. She seemed remarkably untouched by his disappearance, as if Longstaff had planned the whole thing with her connivance. I knew I was vulnerable and, resisting the inclination to relax, I installed a barricade of ice beneath my bland exterior.

However, throughout dinner her behaviour was beyond reproach and inevitably I began to relax again. I won't bore you with details of what we had to eat, but her standards were high and I was impressed with the food and the unpretentious service. When the manservant poured the St Emilion, for example, he did not bother to let me taste it; *she* knew it was good so there was no need for ceremony. Towards the end of the meal we got round to Longstaff in general terms and she was able to answer some of the questions that had puzzled me earlier – especially why his movements during the 24 hours before the discovery of his clothes had been so difficult to trace. Much of the problem, it seemed, stemmed from the relationship between him and his secretary of eighteen years, Hilary Simmons; a relationship of unquestioned trust and discretion. In fact, Miss Simmons should have retired three years earlier, but she was a secretary of the old school to whom job and employer came before anything else in her life. Longstaff appreciated her qualities and refused to replace her while she was able and willing to continue. But because her loyalty to Longstaff took precedence over the company, she was content to accept the fact that he told her only what he wanted to tell her; even that was treated with the utmost discretion. She covered for him when he decided to take a day off, even when she was sure that company business was the last thing on his mind. The result was that entries in his diary were only those that he told her about in advance so that she could make any arrangements that might be necessary for travel or hotel accommodation, and there were as many blanks as entries.

Although Miss Simmons was kindly disposed towards Ellen Longstaff, who had arrived so relatively late on the scene, she retained her customary discretion. Even the most innocent questions were parried if she was not certain that Longstaff would have authorised an answer. And because of her touching faith in Longstaff's omnipotence she never worried if he did not stay in touch. In fact, on the day before his scheduled trip to Hampshire he had taken a day off for what he casually dismissed as "research", but for all she knew he was merely enjoying a much-needed break. But then she considered that was none of her business, nor that of anyone else.

I was feeling sorry for the old harridan by the time Ellen had finished, especially when she pointed out that unless Longstaff suddenly reappeared she would be pensioned off by a company that considered they had already been over-generous in keeping her employed beyond the statutory retirement age.

Diffidently I enquired whether Longstaff had been any more forthcoming with her, or whether that side of his life had been a closed shop.

She reflected, her expression thoughtful. "Anthony was 46 when we married. He never had to answer to anyone. I could hardly expect him to change overnight. I may not always know *where* he is, but at least he always let me know if he was coming home or not ... mainly, I think, because he respects *my* privacy."

"You have your own interests ... ?"

She smiled; our eyes met and the crumbling barrier of ice finally melted. "It would not be disloyal to say that ours was never really a love match. Respect, from the outset, and later affection."

"He was proud of you. He made a point of telling me about your cultural interests ... "

A flicker of surprise showed in her eyes and she took several seconds to digest the information. "Perhaps I should not have been so stunned when your present turned up. I know that he didn't actually go out and choose it – that would have been too much to expect – but it's significant that he realised jewellery was missing the mark."

"I think he eventually realised that he had been taking you for granted. He wasn't alone in that respect. *Most* of us fall into the same trap."

"Speak for yourself," she admonished me, tongue in cheek.

I apologised and pointedly complimented her on the meal before changing the subject and asking if there was something specific she wanted to discuss. "Or did I jump to the wrong conclusion when you invited me over?"

"No, there *was* something; I got carried away. It isn't often I can talk like this, to let my hair down. I'm very fond of my friends at the theatre, but their interests are inclined to be limited, and I've always kept my married life quite separate. They tend to think there's something rather indecent about money and the City ... perhaps they're right ... In fact they still know me by my former name, Farini ... "

"You were married to the Hollywood producer, James Farini?"

She raised her eyebrows. "Do you know him?"

"I used to go to the cinema a lot. I still read the reviews – and the gossip columns."

Her smile was cynical. "The way he's been carrying on lately that's the only place one would read about him now. He hasn't made a decent film for years."

"Didn't he recently do a series of documentaries on the Amazon?"

"As it happens, *they* were quite good. He rode himself in on the back of a damn good director who came up with an original treatment – or perhaps I'm doing him an injustice; perhaps he still has something to offer. His publicity people came up with a story that the great James Farini was tired of prostituting his art and wanted to get to grips with Truth – with a capital T. I know Jimmy well enough to read between the lines. The real truth – with a small t – was that he couldn't raise the cash for another feature film, so documentaries that could be sold to TV were something of a face-saver."

"I didn't realise he was in trouble."

She sighed. "I don't really want to talk about Jimmy. He reminds me too much of my own shortcomings."

I squeezed her hand across the table, wondering if I was overstepping the mark. "I didn't know you had any."

The expression of wide-eyed bewilderment was genuine. "Why do you think I can't keep a husband?"

"You're not suggesting that Longstaff disappeared – to get away from his wife?"

She laughed. "I didn't mean that literally. It was me who left Jimmy, in any case. I meant the inability to learn from my mistakes. My two husbands were like peas from the same pod; both talented in their different ways, single-minded to the point of obsession – and adulterers. Anthony has the edge in brains, of course, although, more to the point, he *thinks* before making a move; in other words, he is not only careful but discreet."

I made no comment but something in my expression prompted her to qualify her observation. "Oh, I know about his reputation with women, but short of employing a private detective which I could never do on principle, I've never been able to catch him out. He's also selective, whereas Jimmy doesn't – or didn't – care a damn. My first husband would not think twice about seducing the wife of his best friend, but forgot that a path littered with cuckolded husbands who also happened to be studio heads, distributors, backers and assorted big wheels in the industry is like a minefield ... if it doesn't kill you, at the very least it obstructs progress."

"You must have been very young when you married him."

"That's enough breast-beating for one day. Let me tell you why I asked you to come. It's about Anthony's books ... "

"Books from the pension fund?"

"I think these must have been Anthony's, although now you come to mention it, I couldn't be sure – as far as I know he never had any books like this of his own ... ?"

"What's the problem?"

"Nothing, I hope. Three days ago, I had a phone call from a man who claimed that Anthony had promised to return two books which he had taken on approval. I said I knew nothing about it and that he would have to wait for my husband to sort it out – but obviously he had read about Anthony in the newspapers and was worried about getting his books back. He said he knew where they would be and that he could produce the carbon of an invoice he had submitted. It seemed satisfactory enough so I invited him over to collect them. I found the books where he said they would be ... "

"Where was that?"

"In a trunk where Anthony keeps some of his private papers. They were beautiful fine bindings, and I was tempted enough to find the money myself, but they were really *too* expensive."

"So you handed them over?"

"I'm probably being unnecessarily suspicious, but I began to wonder what Anthony was doing with them. If he had given you the pension-fund assignment, surely he wouldn't interfere by buying books himself? And what had he done with the top copy of that invoice ... ? He was meticulous about these things."

"Did you get a receipt for the books?"

"They were not our books in the first place; why

should he give me a receipt?"

"What was the bookseller's name?"

She pulled a face. "That's part of the problem. I don't remember. I think it was Horton, but I'm not sure. I think the shop is in Cricklewood. I remember seeing the letterhead but it didn't really register."

I made a note and asked if she could describe the books.

There was relief in her smile. "I couldn't swear to the exact titles but I've still got a reasonably clear picture of the books themselves ... "

"You would make a good bookseller," I commented. "I remember my customers – not by their names, but by the books they buy."

"I don't know about ordinary books – these were exceptional. The one I instantly fell in love with had an inlaid handpainted miniature of Nell Gwynn in a gilt frame inside the front cover. That in turn was set in a sort of gilt frame around the inside edges of the cover ... "

"*Dentelles*," I interjected, my stomach turning with alarm. It was too much of a coincidence not to be the book I had purchased for the pension fund – a superb Sangorski and Sutcliffe bound edition of *The Story of Nell Gwyn* by Peter Cunningham. No wonder Ellen had been captivated. I had paid £800 for it and was confident that there were two collectors among my own customers apart from a specialist dealer who would pay £1000 on sight. Ordinary first editions of the book, first published in 1852, were not uncommon, but this version contained extra illustrations and views, some of which were handpainted. It was bound in red levant morocco, tooled in gold with royal emblems, and the fly-leaves were of silk ... a work of exquisite craftsmanship.

I managed to keep my face expressionless despite the pictures flooding my memory. There was no point in complicating the issue by telling her of my fears. After recovering from her embarrassment she might even feel inclined to go to the police, and I wanted to get at Horton first.

"The other book was in a pigskin box ... it could have been the works of Chaucer, but again it was ..."

I nodded to convey my interest but my mind was racing ahead. This was another of my purchases, presumably not as magnificent as the Kelmscott Press edition which I had never been fortunate enough to see, but an 18th-century masterpiece for which I had paid just over £2000.

What was going on? The only way Horton could have known where the books were was if Longstaff had told him – or shown him – if they had some private deal in books that were not, in any case, the property of either of them. I had to find out.

A phone call to Charlie Appleton at the shop was enough to obtain the information I wanted. The only name that resembled Horton in the North West London section of Sheppard's directory of booksellers was a Stephen Gorton – and that was good enough for me. His shop, just off Cricklewood Broadway, was a shabby, single-fronted premises with an apparently random assortment of odds and ends in a window that could not have been cleaned for years. Even to a bibliophile like myself it required an effort of will to peer through the grime at what amounted to only a handful of volumes, each with a dog-eared price-tag protruding from the closed pages. Behind them, the inside of the shop was hidden by the backs of bookshelves, facing inwards and full enough to act as a screen. The front door was closed and I could see no signs of movement, but there was an arrow pointing to the bell and a typed note sellotaped to the window, reading "please ring". Gorton was presumably the sort of bookseller who did not bother much with the passing trade, relying instead on catalogues.

The place looked so run down and the note was so discoloured by age and the elements that I did not really expect a response, but within seconds the door was opened by a youngish man who might have been mistaken for an artist, not any bookseller I knew. His strikingly blond hair was long but tapered elegantly to his neck and he was wearing a green velvet jacket, red shirt and tan trousers – an incongruously vivid figure against the general shabbiness of the shop. He had a face like a Greek god but the effect was marred by his manner. It wasn't clear at the time whether I had caught him at an inconvenient moment or he was always like that, but the expression indicated that he was far too busy to waste time on casual callers. "I'm afraid we are closed," he announced, his tone almost petulant.

"Mr Gorton?" I enquired brightly. "I am a friend of Mrs Longstaff. She asked me to have a word with you about the books you took the other day ..."

He looked at me distastefully and did not move and, feeling like a high-pressure salesman, I pointedly put a foot on the step and asked if I might come in. He took several seconds before making up his mind and then tossed his head with apparent indifference. I realised he was gay, an impression that was confirmed when he opened the door wider and by his movements when he followed me inside.

While my attitude to homosexuals is ambivalent I found myself studying him carefully. He was about my height, not so heavily built, but had the finely tuned physique of an athlete, and I guessed that he probably spent hours in the gymnasium with the weights. His bone structure was immaculate, something that was not immediately apparent because the colourful dress was a distraction, but he was the sort of Adonis that would attract women in their droves – until they realised they could not interest him.

The shop housing a few thousand run-of-the-mill secondhand books was relatively bare and, although there was a desk, it was obvious he had not been working there when I arrived. "How can I help you, Mr ...?"

I hesitated. If he and Longstaff were running a fraudulent operation, he would know my name, and I was reluctant to put him on his guard. "Cottingham," I announced, giving Laura's name. Since I had spent the night with her, shared a shower and breakfast, I did not feel too bad about borrowing her name in the bargain. "Mrs Longstaff couldn't find the top copy of your invoice. She is worried that when her husband turns up, he will be annoyed with her. She wondered if she might have a receipt from you."

"Why should I give her a receipt for *my* books?"

"*You* know they were your books. She doesn't. What if her husband tells her they were his? Without casting aspersions, it could be a question of your word against his ... ?"

"She can easily clear the point up by checking through the stubs in his cheque-book."

"Of course ... if he were any other man. Unfortunately Longstaff is an entrepreneur. He had at least half a dozen cheque-books; she wouldn't know where to start ..."

He made a token effort to be polite. "I'm sorry, Mr

Cottingham. That's hardly my problem, is it?"

"I wonder if I could just see the books."

He smiled for the first time, but there was a supercilious edge to it. "Pity. They've just been sold."

"*Both* of them? You've got a very healthy business!"

"You don't think I depend on the shop for my living?"

"Obviously not, but I'm a bookseller myself, and I know that the sort of customers who can afford that sort of book – *either* of them – are not so thick on the ground. Were they private collectors ... or institutional bodies ... ?"

"What are you proposing? That we swop names and addresses of our best customers?"

I ignored the sarcasm. "Mrs Longstaff was particularly impressed with the Nell Gwyn binding. Do you have a provenance for it? Or at least the name of the previous owner?"

He looked pointedly at his watch. "I don't see that can be any business of yours. I'm afraid I can't stop now. The printers are chasing me for copy for the next catalogue. Just tell Mrs Longstaff not to worry. If there is any problem at all it can be sorted out in due course between me and her husband."

"Longstaff has bought books from you before, has he?"

"Again, what business is that of yours?"

"None, but let me remind you: I'm speaking on behalf of Mrs Longstaff. Another thing that worries her is that he is not a book-collector, so why would he even contemplate buying two in isolation – especially at the sort of prices on your invoice ... ?"

Gorton seemed to relax imperceptibly. "She has her facts wrong. Mr Longstaff does collect books – on mathematics and early science. Not many, admittedly, but enough to whet his appetite."

I knew that to be at least partially true so I changed tack. "Let's come back to my interest. When I said I was a bookseller I might have added that I represent the Allman & Spinks pension fund, and that I have been buying a number of items on their behalf ... through Mr Longstaff, of course. Did he mention it to you?"

Gorton shook his head.

"You see," I continued with apparent innocence. "By a really remarkable coincidence I recently bought two books which sound absolutely identical. Isn't that amazing?"

He tried to animate the expression of indifference. "It is," he conceded. "Except that *we* both know that what the average person thinks is the same can be different in a whole variety of ways – different edition, quality of binding; different leather, type-face ... you name it."

"Ah, but it's not as simple as that," I remarked. "My copy, that is ... the pension-fund copy, seems to have disappeared ... "

He looked at me blankly and shrugged his shoulders. "So?"

"Mrs Longstaff remembered certain features that are unique, and that means that, despite my conviction that I had bought a *one-off*, either there are two identical copies, or you somehow bought yourself stolen property – inadvertently, of course ... "

Gorton studied me, wondering if I knew anything or was speculating; whether he should continue with his programme of lies, or try to hedge his bets by clouding the issue. While he hesitated I exerted a little more pressure. "That's why the provenance would be invaluable; we could see at a glance."

He nodded. "I can see your point, Mr ... er ... Cottingham. Obviously that makes it a different kettle of fish because it is now in my interest to find out. I will, even if it means turning the place upside down."

I smiled reassuringly. "Good. I'll help you."

There was obviously nothing in the shop and I moved towards an open door leading to an inner room. He thrust an arm across the doorway to bar my path. "The place is in a mess. I explained that I'm working on a catalogue. I'll ring you with the information later."

I toyed with the idea of insisting, but did not see how I could accomplish anything, short of violence, if he retained his stance. I stared at his arm stretched in front of me like an iron bar. Gorton's jacket sleeve and shirt cuff were pulled back and I was conscious of the smooth skin of his forearm ... not a single hair to be seen on his arm or on the back of his wrist. It was like a woman's hand. The image brought back another memory and I remembered my assailant in the Allman & Spinks conference room. I had found him again.

The realisation came as a shock, but I was quite sure so there was nothing to say. He already knew who I really was, but now we were on equal terms. I would give him as much advance warning as he had given me. I brought my heel down sharply on his instep and, as he stepped back involuntarily, swept the hard edge of my stiffened hand in a swinging arc to his face. Considering it was a blow I had not practised for years I was relieved to see it land spot on – against the upper lip, at the base of his nose. He was unconscious before he hit the ground and I had to step over him into what looked like a workroom. There was a slight throbbing in my right forearm, but I knew the cuts had healed properly and relaxed again.

A bench in the centre of the room was littered with strips of leather, three or four books and binders' tools, and I could see at a glance that he was a craftsman of some skill. Right in the middle of the bench was the evidence he had not wanted me to find – the miniature painting on ivory of Nell Gwyn, out of its frame, and alongside it a colour photographic likeness on art paper already set in a metal frame. Gorton had constructed an attractive but cheap copy of my masterpiece; but from a distance it could be passed off as the original.

He was beginning to stir so I found the kitchen, filled a coffee-mug with cold water and used it to bring him to his senses. Still sprawled in the doorway, he looked up at me defiantly, but he could not hold my stare; the fight had been knocked out of him. I lifted a foot within an inch of his nose. "You're a good-looking chap, Stephen, but a squashed nose would be something of a drawback, don't you think?"

He touched his nose gingerly. "It feels like you've broken it already."

"On the contrary, I was very precise – I missed your nose deliberately. Pain can be disorientating."

He looked worried by my apparent expertise in the matter, but said nothing; it was clear I was firmly in the driving-seat. I told him what I had seen on the work bench, and demanded: "What do you do with the copies when you've made them?"

"They go to Longstaff's collection ... "

"The pension-fund collection ... ? And the originals?"

"We sell them ... "

"*We*?"

"I do the dirty work, and get 20% of the split. He

takes the rest."

"Was that the plan from the outset?" He nodded. "So that's why I had to submit the lists. Presumably it was you who made the decisions. You turned down anything that could not be replaced by replicas ... by a copy in this instance, or cheaper editions of the first ..."

He nodded again. "We had to buy and keep some originals for the sake of appearances. Usually we would turn down specials or limited editions; the Nell Gwyn was an exception because it was easy to fabricate – at least, if it was kept under glass one wouldn't look too closely."

I was staggered by the scale of their fraud. "Surely you didn't expect to get away with it?"

"Why not? The collection was supposed to remain under lock and key and we were careful about outward appearances – so no-one was likely to check until the fund ever got round to selling the collection, and Longstaff would make sure that wasn't for at least 15 to 20 years."

"How much did you both expect to make?"

Gorton made an effort to regain his composure. "I'm not going to incriminate myself by saying anything more."

I shrugged. "Relax ... Apart from the Nell Gwyn material on the work bench, the evidence is pretty sketchy. It's basically my word against yours."

"Exactly, and I'll deny everything."

"Exactly," I echoed.

"You don't seem terribly concerned?"

"Curious," I conceded, "and fascinated by your ingenuity. Do you know if Longstaff was doing anything similar with his other projects?"

"If you knew the guy you wouldn't ask such a

stupid question … he wouldn't let his left hand know what his right was doing … "

"If he was, he would have been making a fortune on the side. Well enough from this alone … ?" I looked at him expectantly but he did not rise to the bait, so I continued. "It's not difficult to estimate. I was given a budget of £300,000 and he made a point of saying he did not want too many cheaper books – despite the fact they have a higher growth potential. Like the total innocent I fell for his excuse of not wanting to start a vast library. Now it's obvious he was thinking of your problems of trying to resell them … "

"I've said all I'm saying," Gorton replied, avoiding my eyes.

" … An average price of around £1000 would involve 300 books. That cuts the number down substantially, but doesn't necessarily make it any easier because of the higher unit value … ?"

Gorton laughed at my attempts to draw him out. "If you imagine I'm so full of my own cleverness that I can't wait to confess everything, you're going to be disappointed. I can't stop you speculating … and you can't make me confirm or deny anything … "

I shrugged. "I can work it out for myself. Let's say you've got one or two friends in the trade who don't ask too many questions. You would have to give them a substantial discount … say *half*? Never mind, that is detail which doesn't matter. We'll *say* half price, which is an average of £500 … multiplied by 300 … equals £150,000 … " I had consciously ignored his comment earlier about keeping some originals "for the sake of appearances", but he made no effort to correct me, so I continued. "From that gross figure you would have to deduct the cost of your replacements – let's allow £50 a time to include the cost of materials for any cosmetic frills that might be needed ... that leaves a net profit of £135,000 ... "

The smile had disappeared. "I don't see much evidence of that sort of wealth around here."

"You admitted that 80% of that went to Longstaff. Besides, appearances are deceptive. I would never have dreamt that the guy in denim overalls was a *fairy* like you ... "

My clumsy attempt to goad him misfired and the smile returned. "Blue rather suits me, actually ... "

I returned his smile. "I'm sure it does. Pity you had to spoil the effect with the stocking mask. One of yours, was it?"

"Fully fashioned, my dear."

"Presumably you got worried when Longstaff disappeared, and decided to get back some of the fakes. You knew about my regular visits from him ... "

He shrugged petulantly.

"All right, forget it. What about Longstaff ... do you know where he is?"

"No. If I had to guess, I would say Brazil."

I took the ivory-mounted painting and his photographic copy, with a few strips of the red leather he had intended to use. "I'm keeping these for the time being," I announced. "I won't hand them over to the police ... for now, unless you also decide to do a bunk."

He got to his feet and brushed his clothes fastidiously. He avoided looking at me and I sensed that he was thinking of getting his own back. There were some nasty-looking tools on the work bench and he was obviously fit and strong, but I wasn't worried about handling him face-to-face. I made a point of not turning my back and when our eyes met, I shook my head in a silent warning and he got the message.

Outside again I took a deep breath. I had learned a lot, but much more important – where did I go from here?

Seven

The showdown with Gorton left me in something of a quandary. By not going to the police with the evidence I had uncovered I was technically an accessory after the fact, yet I was not prepared to lose any sleep over it. My reasons were complex. For a start, there were pieces of the puzzle still missing and, now that I had made the breakthrough, I did not want outsiders taking over. Perhaps if Inspector Murdoch had been involved my attitude might have been different – he would not try to shut me out – but, in the present circumstances, no-one was going to deny me the opportunity of completing what I considered a very personal commitment.

To strengthen my resolve, there was also a sense of loyalty to Longstaff that surprised even myself. In his eyes, I was merely a pawn he could manipulate – which was not easy for my pride to stomach, yet obviously there was nothing personal in his exploitation of me and others, and in my innocence I had stood to earn a large sum of money. This awareness alone was enough to stop me rushing off to the authorities without, at least, learning his side of the story – preferably from his own mouth. Ellen also came into the reckoning. Having uncovered a fraud, Allman & Spinks might demand that the pension fund be compensated from Longstaff's estate, and I did not want to make her a victim of his greed.

Although I felt free to keep my options open, I was reluctant to take the added responsibility on my shoulders alone. Sharing the new information might not only lessen the burden but possibly produce some form of hitherto unexpected assistance. There were only two people directly involved that I knew well enough to confide in – Ellen and David Morgan. I felt that Ellen probably merited prior consideration, although there was little in it. Admittedly, there was a risk she might ask me to remain silent whatever the outcome – something I could not promise in advance – but I could face that problem if and when it arose.

In any case, when in doubt I tend to allow 'fate' to decide my course of action, so it seemed logical since I was in Cricklewood to drive to Ellen first, and if she was not readily available to go on to Portman Square where I would talk to Morgan. I suspected she was probably at the theatre, but as her home was first in line on the road map I made a slight detour to see if her red Mini Clubman was outside. As I had more or less expected, it was not there – but there was another car, the latest model BMW 528i. The road was a restricted parking area with special meters for residents, so it was unlikely that the owner of the huge silver-grey BMW lived in the road or was visiting another property, and yet it seemed equally unlikely there was anyone at home. I hesitated over stopping to find out; after all, the owner of an expensive car like that was hardly a burglar, and if Ellen Longstaff had a visitor it was none of my business. Yet I was curious, and since I was actually on the spot ... I decided to wait to see who emerged; I would allow fifteen minutes, unless a traffic warden came along first. I pulled up on the opposite side of the road, some 25 yards to the rear.

No-one appeared. Inevitably I gave it another five minutes and then, having waited so long, another. However, that was where I drew the line and I was on the point of giving up when the Longstaff's front door opened and a middle-aged man came out – at least, 'middle-aged' was the impression I got from a distance, heightened by the tailored fawn top-coat with velvet collar he was wearing – hardly the style of a young man. Then I lost interest in him, because he was followed out by Ellen's daughter Jacintha.

I suppose I should not have been so surprised to see the girl; after all, this was obviously where she lived – but when she kissed him on the lips the tableau assumed an air of intrigue. Usually I'm loath to jump to conclusions, but there seemed little doubt she had been entertaining a lover. The stranger was considerably older than her, of course, but as he went to his car, moving closer into focus, I could see, judging by the cut of his clothes and his new car, that he was well-groomed and well-heeled, and I knew Jacintha was impressed by the trappings of success.

When the BMW drove off I decided I could not face Ellen yet. There was something underhand about her daughter's relationship with the stranger. If he only called when Jacintha was alone, it implied there was a reason for secrecy; the immediate implication being that the man was married. Annoyed at having wasted so much time, I brushed the Longstaffs from my thoughts and headed for town where I told my story of the meeting with Gorton to David Morgan. He listened without interruption, his face getting longer by the minute. When I had finished he asked what I intended to do with the information. When I shrugged, he smiled: "You're as bad as me."

I raised a questioning eyebrow.

"At playing God ... placing ourselves above the law ..."

I realised what he was getting at. "Don't tell me you've also been keeping something under your hat?"

He nodded. "I found two or three what might best be called 'irregularities', but I've been sitting on the information. My loyalties are torn between the company that employs me and Anthony Longstaff, because he always took an interest in me. That doesn't excuse the way he seems to have behaved, But I think Ellen Longstaff has suffered enough without learning about this too."

I noticed that he flushed slightly when he mentioned her name, and suspected I was not alone in appearing to have a rapport with Ellen Longstaff. The difference was that he was already concealing information specifically to protect her; I doubted whether I could go that far when all the facts were available.

I hinted as much. "By all means let ignorance be bliss for the moment, but we may not be able to keep this under wraps for ever. Seems to me the only person who has all the answers is Longstaff, and even if he is still alive, I can't see him turning up now just to satisfy our curiosity. What do you think?"

"Nothing would surprise me any more. I always admired the man. I never imagined he would turn out to be such a selfish sod ... "

"Selfish?"

"What else? He was not the sort of man to do *anything* on the spur of the moment. If he really intended to commit suicide he would have given that as much preparatory thought as any important business project ... "

"What has that got to do with it?"

"You probably didn't know he had a life-insurance policy for £200,000 ... ?" Without waiting for a reaction, he continued: "But if they never find his body, Ellen will have one hell of a battle to get *anything* out of it."

I quite liked Morgan. We had not known each other for long but he was down-to-earth, diligent, and if a trifle too earnest, at least he seemed genuine. I hesitated over putting the boot in, but his disclosure of the life-insurance policy, and particularly the size of it, raised other unpleasant possibilities. "If Longstaff is not dead, but can remain out of sight for long enough, the *courts* can take that decision, after so many years – seven, I think it is. There is not much the insurance company can do without any concrete evidence to the contrary; there is more than one precedent. That could easily mean that he is taking his ease somewhere in South America or Australia with a reasonably clear conscience. He might even have warned his wife – after all, no-one could pretend that she is exactly broken-hearted ... "

"Because she hasn't gone into mourning?"

I ignored the implied protest. "On the other hand, if I worked for an insurance company, I could not discount a third possibility – that he was murdered."

Morgan visibly struggled to retain his composure. "That Ellen murdered her husband for a few thousand pounds?"

"*Few* thousand? I echoed. "Forget your personal feelings, David; try to stay detached, to look at the possibilities from outside."

"*You* are an outsider, more or less. Do *you* think she is the type – "

"Type? Are there types?"

" – to kill for money?" he spluttered, ignoring my interruption. "Money is not important to her. You only have to look at the job she does for a pittance."

"Money is not important to me either, but let's keep it in perspective. Ellen can *afford* to work for nothing. And why should our insurance investigator care a damn about her philosophy – or how she chooses to spend her time? He is taught to regard premature payouts as a drain on his own life-blood, so any beneficiary of a policy where the circumstances are not clear-cut automatically comes under suspicion. By the time he had put a magnifying-glass to her background even Florence Nightingale would be a candidate for the hangman ... "

"He can dig up whatever he likes – but he'll find no *evidence*, because there isn't any."

"Don't underestimate these characters. They start by looking for a motive. It would not be difficult for them to find out about Longstaff's infidelities; and it would be a reasonable assumption that his wife had also found out. You know the old adage about Hell having no fury ... ? Once they had made that deduction, it no longer seems such a jump to cast her in the role of the potential murderer who would find £200,000 ample consolation for the heartache she had suffered at her husband's hands."

Morgan shrugged. "It needs a twisted mind."

"Why? Meanwhile, tell me something? Do you merely admire Ellen from afar – or have you declared your affections? More to the point, have they been reciprocated?"

He seemed to be preoccupied with scratching his ear. Several seconds elapsed before he faced me and begged the question. "Depends on who wants to know – friend or insurance investigator?"

I smiled. "Friend. But you don't have to answer. I just wanted to remind you that most wives who murder their husbands have had the assistance of a lover – so in case anyone starts speculating along these lines, you had better stop wearing your heart on your sleeve."

"Is it that obvious?" he asked.

"Look, if you are convinced that Ellen had nothing to do with Longstaff's disappearance – let alone his death – wouldn't it be in our interest to find out what really happened?"

"Of course, but what can we do? Presumably the police haven't been idle."

"You and I have the advantage of being on the inside track. With very little effort I've already uncovered one lead. Unfortunately it doesn't take us very far because I'm pretty sure that Gorton knows nothing about Longstaff's vanishing act. In fact, he must be scared stiff that I'll let the cat out of the bag because quite apart from the drying up of a lucrative source of income, the fakes in the pension-fund collection make him very vulnerable. But you said before *you* were sitting on something new ... what is it?"

He shook his head. "Nothing concrete ... little more than my intuition. But it might at least tell us where Longstaff was on the day before he disappeared ... "

The surge of optimism that showed in my face prompted him to add a note of caution. "Don't raise your hopes too much; it's nothing particularly significant. Certainly not sinister."

"*Anything* ... " I pleaded.

"It's a tape-recording made at Longlands of a business discussion between Longstaff and an American. I don't know the voice but from the discussion I'm reasonably certain it was James Farini, Ellen's former husband. I haven't said anything to her yet because she would have been upset – she dislikes him intensely. She would have been stunned that they were meeting behind her back, even though the reason was strictly business."

"How could you pinpoint the date when the tape was recorded?"

"I couldn't swear to it, but the cassette was still in the machine. I found out Longstaff's movements – apart from the one day that we couldn't account for – the day off he told his secretary he was using for 'research'. It seems he was. The tape was a discussion about the possibility of the pension fund investing in a new film Farini is producing."

I recalled Ellen's remarks about Farini's short-comings as a film producer, but since I did not know whether she had mentioned our tête-à-tête to Morgan I decided not to raise the matter in case he was jealous. Instead, I asked if I could listen to the tape.

Morgan rummaged in his desk drawer for a cassette. "I should explain that Longstaff was in the habit of recording practically all private business discussions so that he could double-check on precisely what had been said at any particular point. Miss Simmons has several dozen filed in the other room, but I also knew he kept a concealed recorder at Longlands. I suspect he used it for other things too ... he admitted he was turned on by listening to women with whom he made love – shall we say 'on heat' – and although I can't be sure he used it to record himself in the sex act, I do know he had quite a collection of professional sound and video tapes. That is really how this tape came to light. I didn't think Ellen knew about the pornography so I thought I could kill two birds with one stone by getting her permission to go down there and sort through his files ... "

"Do you mean to say the police didn't go through the place with a toothcomb?"

"They went through the motions. To be fair, they had no idea what they were looking for. As far as they were concerned, it was a country house that Longstaff visited only occasionally, except in the heart of summer. It was a place where he came to relax. What they could not possibly know was that since he never stopped working, pleasure was never really divorced from business – or the other way round."

"But what about the tape you've got there? Didn't they even play that?"

He laughed. "Luckily it was Ellen who showed them round, and they were probably a little embarrassed over the invasion of privacy at a time like that ... she was still pretty shocked. They looked in a few cupboards, but what no-one knew – except me – was that when he did not want to be disturbed, Longstaff used what he called the library – where Ellen keeps her books. Because it was really her room they barely glanced inside ... " He shrugged expressively.

Morgan had produced a portable cassette recorder from the large side drawer of his desk and loaded it. Then he paused, as though to introduce the recording we were about to hear. "As I said, I found this in the machine concealed in a cocktail cabinet. It had run out before the end of the meeting, but presumably he had already made his decision – which made it unnecessary to continue – and did not bother to turn it over, or whatever it was he used to do."

"Nor bother to remove it later?"

"He probably left with his guest ... " Morgan

pressed the 'play' button and there was a faint hissing as the tape began to move. He looked at me apologetically. "I don't have a Dolby on this machine, but the voices are clear enough ... "

Before he had completed his apology my stomach began to flutter nervously. The sound of Longstaff's voice made it seem as though we were conducting a séance and his spirit was in the room with us.

" ... Cosier in here ... "

"Incredible view ... " The other voice had a cultured American accent and I had an instant mental picture of the broadcaster Alistair Cooke. Determinedly I wiped the picture clean and took a firm hold of my imagination, but at that moment Morgan brought me down to earth by speeding up the tape, pointing out that we did not need to listen to several minutes of waffle and aimless pleasantries. He recommenced with the start of the more relevant section.

"So you are looking for money ... " Longstaff made it a statement, but as casual as though he was talking about the weather.

I was conscious of the sounds made by the leather armchairs I had found so comfortable, and tried to visualise them take their ease. There was a throaty chuckle from Longstaff's visitor. "I don't know how to answer that," he conceded. "I can always get money, but obviously I would not be here today if I was totally independent. I've got half a dozen loyal backers I can always rely on for a few thousand here and a few thousand there. Unfortunately, for this project that is peanuts. My distributors have told me that if I can raise $6 million – up front – they will match it. It's an offer I can't refuse ... "

"Of course not. Sounds pretty generous to me."

There was another chuckle. "It's a fairly common ploy. They know that any project that can raise that sort of *up-front* money must be gilt-edged. If I told them I only needed $50,000 they would be highly suspicious. What kind of rubbish can Farini be making for peanuts, they would ask themselves."

"I can understand. $6 *million* is hardly peanuts, even for us."

"It doesn't have to be the *whole* shooting match, but I'm looking to you – or one of your competitors – to set the ball rolling with something substantial ... $4 or 5 million would be fantastic ..."

"Still a lot of money ..."

"Surely not by present-day standards? Besides, film backing has become respectable. Your National Coal Board pension fund coughed up near enough $1 million for a smaller project not so long ago and I reckon they have already doubled their investment."

"Obviously I watch these things with interest. The actual figure was $400,000 ... a bit less than you were told ... and it was not for one film but a series. Furthermore they knew in advance it would sell to television throughout the world."

"Which is precisely what *we* expect, although ours' is a much bigger kettle of fish altogether. Despite the sum involved, we expect to be in profit after the initial movie sales in the United States. On top of that will be overseas sales ... before we even look at television, which is as big again."

"Well it's heartening to hear such confidence but you know what we money-men are like. We are less impressed by forecasts than by box-office receipts."

"Of course. I don't expect you to take anything on trust, or even to be influenced by my track record – although that's not bad at all, if I say so myself. What you cannot ignore though is the script. It's adapted from the best-selling novel *Red Dawn*. I don't know whether the title means much to you, but it was a *smash* ... made the author a millionaire ... it's even been translated into Japanese. Why else would I be talking about a $12 million budget. There are three male leads and I've got Redford, De Niro and Clint Eastwood lined up – any one of whom could pull the sort of money I'm talking about ... What a mix!"

"That makes quite a difference," conceded Longstaff. "If you have a firm commitment from them, I don't need to know much else."

"*Mad* keen. Absolutely champing at the bit – all of them."

"But no *contracts* yet?"

"Not at *this* stage, of course. But I've spoken to all three – or their agents – and they are so keen we're not even going to have problems with billing."

"Quite something."

"Guys like that are not fools. They know a story like this only comes up once in a lifetime."

"But they won't actually commit themselves?"

"Take it from me, each and every one of them will bust a gut to make himself available, but even the biggest star can't afford to hang about for a couple of years until *we* are ready to shoot."

"What about the female leads?"

"The big box-office draws are men, so I'm not bothered. We can get whoever we like. In fact, *you* name her and I promise to deliver."

From the tone of his voice, Longstaff seemed amused. "I wouldn't dream of interfering. I'm a money-man. I know nothing about film-making. My policy is to trust in the experts ... "

"That's how it should be. Look ... do you mind if I

call you Tony? I'm not a man to mix business with pleasure, and I'm sure you are not, but I've got pencilled in two or three fantastic actresses who would give their virginities – if they still had them – for a part in this film. You don't need me to tell you how grateful they are going to be when we give them the good news – grateful to me, *and* to my friends and colleagues ... "

"Gratitude is a virtue we don't see enough of these days," said Longstaff, "but I'm afraid balance-sheets have to remain my priority – no matter how tempting the diversions. Hadn't you better show me some projected figures?"

I heard the snap of locks on an attaché-case as, presumably, the American produced his budgets. There was some rustling of paperwork as he handed it over. "I can't leave it with you today," he announced, "but take as long as you like and if you are still interested I'll have copies made."

There was a silence for several seconds and eventually Longstaff offered his guest a drink. "It will take me a while to plough through this properly, so why don't you have a whisky?"

The American chuckled. "Great minds ... I've brought my own and I insist you try that. I was going to save it for a celebration drink when we close the deal, but to hell with formality ... "

"What happens if we don't close the deal?"

"We'll see. Maybe I'll pour what's left in your glass back in the bottle. It's the best malt whisky in the world – I wouldn't want to waste it on people not on my wavelength. Or maybe I'll take the hint and go back and do some sums."

"I recognise the label, but I must admit I haven't tried it. I'm rather conservative ... stick to the same brand."

"Well I'll try yours if you try mine."

Longstaff laughingly agreed and I heard the sound of liquid being poured into separate glasses.

"Cheers."

"Salut."

There was silence for several minutes, and Morgan speeded up the tape, explaining that Longstaff had taken about fifteen minutes to study the documents and there had been no sound apart from pages being turned and the drinks being replenished. When we picked up the discussion again, Longstaff cleared his throat and asked: "Did you do this presentation yourself?"

"Is it *that* obvious?"

"Not really. It's just that after all these years I've developed a *feel* for figures ... the way some people read handwriting. It doesn't read like the work of a trained accountant ... no disrespect intended."

"None taken. I was going to hand it over to my accountant, but it's such a personal project that I want to be involved in everything. I would even direct and act in it – if I didn't know better. Anything wrong?"

"Nothing that can't be attributed to your natural enthusiasm. For example, I can't find any provision here for the inevitable production hold-ups ... "

"You'll find it under 'contingencies'."

"That is merely a rounding-up figure. There are three overseas locations, including one in the Far East. You can hardly expect to come through completely untouched by bad weather, illness, and strikes. Even *revolution* in one of these countries ..."

"I've also included a figure for insurance. That covers most things."

There was a cynical laugh from Longstaff. "I would

need to read the small print of that policy. In any case, while I do not question your knowledge of how long the filming should take, I'm worried about the amount of travel. Seems you have left very little margin for error. Obviously much depends on the director; who do you have in mind?"

"The best, Hugo Dahrendorf."

"Didn't he get an Oscar about three years ago?"

There was surprise in the American's voice. "Hey! You said you knew nothing about films."

"About film *production*," corrected Longstaff. "I've always been interested in films. Besides, I always do my homework before a meeting like this. Didn't I read that Dahrendorf brought his last two films in several million dollars over budget?"

"He needs a strong hand – like me."

"Hmm. But you can't spend all your time looking over his shoulder. As it stands now – with all these imponderables – I'm afraid I think it's a risk I would be irresponsible to take."

"What if I was to get another director?"

"By all means try me again. In the meantime I think I would prefer to stay in the areas in which I have a little more experience. I must admit I was tempted. I'm sure it would have been an interesting experience."

"Don't make a snap judgement; sleep on it. You could come on location yourself ... keep an eye on your investment ... keep us *all* in check."

"Better say 'no'. Perhaps I can arrange one or two introductions ... No hard feelings, I hope?"

"None at all! Let's drink to that ... "

There was no more dialogue on the tape, only a few miscellaneous sound effects before the click of the cassette running out.

"So that was Farini?" I enquired.

"Too much of a coincidence not to be," said Morgan. "It was common knowledge that Longstaff was broadening his investment spread, so why shouldn't Farini make the approach?"

I had found the tape interesting, although it probably had little relevance to what we were after. However, something was better than nothing. I suggested that Morgan paid Farini a visit. "If nothing else it narrows the gap in time, especially if they came back to London together."

"I wonder why Farini hasn't come forward ... and told the police or even Ellen," Morgan reflected.

"Something you might ask him. Perhaps he has."

"Probably wouldn't want it known he had been after finance and been turned down."

"On the contrary, what is to stop him cashing in on the publicity? Claiming that Longstaff had promised to back him – and what a blow it has been to lose all that finance ... no-one could deny it."

"Of course, there is a more sinister reason for keeping quiet," speculated Morgan. "If he was the last person to see Longstaff, perhaps he knows a lot more. You wouldn't like to come with me?"

He made the request with a smile and I was tempted, but there was a bookshop to run. I pointed out that it would be difficult to justify my presence; nor had I even the right to listen to a disclosure of Farini's private affairs. "You are representing Allman & Spinks, which gives you the right to listen to that tape. I suppose he could have murdered Longstaff, but we would have to establish a better motive than frustration – unless there was a robbery at Longlands which no-one has noticed. Furthermore, what would he have done with the body?"

Morgan shrugged. “Well, perhaps if I ask him nicely he’ll confess. I’ll let you know.”

“Look after yourself,” I said instinctively, as one does without thinking and not really meaning it. “And remember what I said about Ellen Longstaff. Don’t start sending her red roses, and be careful what you say in public.”

He smiled sheepishly. “Thanks, Matt. I know you mean well, but you don’t have to worry about me; and Ellen has got nothing to hide. I know her and I’d trust her with my life.”

“I’m sure that faith is justified,” I replied. “Nothing we’ve said today need be kept from her, so I’ll rely on your discretion, but don’t say anything about Farini. Let’s keep that to ourselves for the moment ...”

He nodded and we parted company. It was the last time I ever saw David Morgan.

Eight

The death of David Morgan came as a body blow. To say that it was unexpected is an understatement; it was more like a mugger sneaking up from behind and scaring the daylights out of you. I’m talking now of the way I heard about it, although even when I had recovered from the initial shock the depression still refused to budge.

I had been preoccupied with work. Despite Charlie Appleton’s efficiency, I could not expect him to come into the shop more than a couple of times a week. Officially, he had retired, and I did not want to take advantage of his willingness; nor could I really afford the privilege of extra time off. It meant by allowing myself to become too involved in "extramural" interests, such as the pension fund, I had to put in extra hours to compensate. People seldom appreciate the amount of behind-the-scenes activity – the time-consuming chore of buying stock for example.

Yet although I was up to my eyes over the next week making up for lost time, David's proposed visit to James Farini was never far from my thoughts and it was not long before I began to champ at the bit for news. When *I* want to meet or interview someone I find it difficult to contain my impatience, and I had to remind myself that David Morgan was not a free agent; that Allman & Spinks kept him fully occupied. However, after a week I began to suspect that he had had second thoughts and that we would never discover the circumstances in which Farini and Longstaff had parted company. I could not *make* him go, but I did consider I was owed an explanation.

When I rang David's office I was asked if it was a personal or a company matter and instead of being put through to him or his secretary I found myself speaking to a man whose voice I did not recognise. Apparently he did not know me either and, from the guarded way he enquired if he could 'help', I got the impression he was an assistant keen to exercise his authority, yet cautious about overstepping the mark – like an assistant bank manager flexing his muscles while the boss is away. The thought irritated me slightly and I reminded him rather pompously that I had asked for David Morgan.

When I repeated my name and referred to my brief for the pension fund, his attitude changed. "Sorry, the switchboard didn't identify you. I'm Chris Jenkins, from Public Relations. Anything other than routine calls are being put through to me for the time being. You obviously haven't heard the news ... "

I was still bewildered, although the thought did cross my mind that Morgan had been sacked ... but that did not make sense either. I settled for a guarded "What news?"

He continued to feel his way. "I don't know if you were friendly with Mr Morgan, but I'm afraid I've got some bad news. He had an accident ... "

I knew from the tone of his voice that the accident had been fatal, and when – almost accusingly – I demanded to know what had happened it was an instinctive reaction because my emotions were in total confusion and I was incapable of thinking rationally. As they jostled for some sort of order, foremost was a sense of loss. There was also irritation at the way I had been kept in ignorance – as though Morgan's death did not merit a phone call – especially on learning that it had happened five days before.

It was not until Jenkins explained the circumstances – that David Morgan had been knocked down by a car that had failed to stop – that the storm in my head passed, leaving a cold anger. Whatever the official version it was suddenly clear to me that it was no accident. The police report indicated that David had been jogging late at night not far from his home, and the driver of the car which struck him may not even have seen his victim because of the relatively poor street lighting. What was far more significant to me was that it happened so soon after David's declared intention to visit Farini. If Farini had killed David because he had something to hide, then the odds were in favour of his having also killed Longstaff.

Concern kept my anger in check. If I had accompanied David as he had asked, he might have been alive now. What I felt was not only a sense of responsibility, but an apprehension that if Farini had covered his tracks well, the police would have no grounds for suspecting that this was not yet another hit-and-run case; that somewhere a panic-stricken motorist was even now trying to come to terms with his conscience. I knew that even if I went to a friend like Inspector Murdoch, there was as yet nothing that the police would regard as evidence to support my allegation. Fortunately I was not a moralist, inhibited by the trappings of the law; I was interested in justice, and with revenging the death of a friend.

My preoccupation cut out Jenkins's voice for a few moments, causing me to miss some of the background information, but I gathered that no-one had come forward in response to a police request for witnesses, and that an inquest had already been opened and adjourned. Despite my anxiety to get at Farini, to beat the truth out of him if necessary, I realised it would be more prudent to prepare my course.

I knew that David Morgan had been a bachelor, and judging by his strong feelings for Ellen Longstaff it was reasonable to assume that he had no other attachments. It never ceases to surprise me how little we know generally about friends and acquaintances outside our immediate circle, and David's background was no exception. I now discovered that he lived at home in Ealing with his widowed mother and that he had just the one brother who had emigrated to Australia some years before. Jenkins told me that he had been to see Mrs Morgan on behalf of the company. "Taken it very well," he reported, "typically English ... stiff upper lip and all that. Nice woman."

I tried to visualise the meeting but only succeeded in

conjuring up a caricature of a very old and frail white-haired lady. I wondered whether her other son had flown back from Australia, or whether she was alone at home, friendless and desolate in her loss. The thought reminded me of Ellen and made me wonder if she had been in touch with Mrs Morgan ... why she had not contacted *me* for that matter ... on reflection whether she even knew of his death. "Presumably it didn't make the papers?," I speculated aloud.

"Only the London evening paper when the police appealed for witnesses. A hit-and-run is hardly news these days."

If the *Standard* had carried just a brief notice, then Ellen should have seen it, or it would have been drawn to her attention – if only because of the reference to Allman & Spinks. In any case, if she and David Morgan were as close as he had implied, it seemed unlikely that a week could elapse without one or other of them getting in touch with the other. I wondered momentarily whether she too had something to hide, whether she was too upset – or whether, apart from the usual platitudes, she merely considered there was little to be said now.

Forcing myself to pay more attention to Jenkins, I asked precisely where the accident had happened. The news that it had been little more than 50 yards from Morgan's home conjured up frightful pictures that it might have been seen by his mother, but he reassured me. "In any case, she had gone to bed. There were no means of identification on the body, and it was not until next morning that a local copper identified him."

I asked for the address, saying that I would like to write to Mrs Morgan; in fact, I intended to call to offer my condolences. Even if I learned nothing of value it would at least ensure that I was in the right mood to confront Farini.

Later I realised I could not just burst in on Farini like the angel of death. Even if he was conveniently alone, if I got too rough he might call my bluff and phone the police. Deciding that a little guile was in order, I telephoned, posing as a feature writer on the Daily Chronicle, and announced that I wanted to write a 'profile' on him as a film artist. Knowing that he was desperately searching for finance, I assumed that he would regard the publicity as heaven-sent and that I could pressure him into an early meeting (I did not want to risk him phoning the Chronicle to postpone our date if something more important cropped up). My luck was in. We arranged to meet at his house in Hampstead the following afternoon.

Trusting that Mrs Morgan was not going anywhere, I phoned her next and arranged to call in for mid-morning coffee. As it happened, Charlie Appleton was not available at such short notice, but trusting that it would not be busy I secured my first 'reserve' assistant, Betty Hardacre, wife of the local newspaper editor.

Jane Morgan lived in a bright, pre-war 'semi' near Ealing Common to the West of London, not far from the airport. After the way my imagination had run riot I was disconcerted to find an attractive, dark-haired woman in her late fifties; tall for her sex and slimly built. The family resemblance was quite strong and it was not difficult to imagine she must have been quite a beauty only a few years before. The eyes were tired and slightly swollen, and it was obvious she had not been sleeping well, but she was in control of her emotions. She obviously meant it when she said how pleased she was to meet any friend of her son.

The conversation over coffee was surprisingly

uninhibited. Mrs Morgan told me that her older son, Geoffrey, wanted her to go back to Australia with him, but she was too fond of her job to give it up until she had to retire. Later, when she began to talk about David, I was frank about the short period of our acquaintanceship, but she did not seem surprised. "In the last five years his job came first, and that meant he lost touch with his friends, especially those that got married. The job was very demanding, with a lot of travelling. Even when he was in London he would be quite exhausted when he came home at night ... "

"I know the firm thought very highly of him," I said. "I suppose that is the price of ambition."

"But *what* a price!" she responded. "David was earning good money, but what did he have to show for it, and for all those long hours? No wife or family of his own; not even any real friends left ... "

I felt I had to say something to alleviate the gloom in some way. "For what it's worth," I remarked, "he wasn't entirely alone. He mentioned someone he was very fond of ... who reciprocated his feelings ... at least, I think she did ... "

She smiled at my discretion. "I think I know who you mean. David hinted as much, although he never actually spoke about her. I can only assume she is married. I suppose something is better than nothing."

I nodded. "We don't all have the same criteria for evaluating happiness. A special relationship outside marriage can be better than an uninspired one that survives only because of convention."

"I never thought of it that way. I'm old-fashioned enough to think of marriage and children as a priority. But I concede he must have loved this woman ... I think he would have done anything for her."

"Did she ever ring him here?"

"Occasionally, when she was confident *he* would answer the phone. In fact, she even rang on the night he died."

My pulse-rate began to quicken. "Earlier in the evening?"

"No, as a matter of fact it was very late; in fact I had just gone up to bed. I wondered if anything was the matter, or whether perhaps they quarrelled ... if it upset David in any way – at least, enough to prevent him from seeing the car that hit him ... "

"I doubt it," I said quickly, to reassure her. "Not that it matters now, anyway, but when *I'm* jogging my mind is always active – it keeps me from noticing the stitch ... "

"David wasn't actually jogging at the time; he had finished his training for the night."

I was taken aback. "That's not the impression I got from the police report ... "

"He had *been* jogging," Mrs Morgan insisted. "And he was still wearing his track suit. He was about to take a shower when the phone rang, and then he called up to me that he was going out again, but wouldn't be long. He used the expression 'popping out' so I took him at his word. I didn't think any more of it and fell asleep."

If her memory was not playing tricks, the phone call was crucial. "What did the police think?"

She looked confused. "About the phone call?"

I nodded encouragingly.

"I didn't mention it; it didn't arise. When they came round, it was merely to break the news about the hit-and-run. He was found in his track suit so they assumed he had been out running. I don't think they even asked me ... or if they did, I may even have confirmed that impression without really thinking.

Why does it matter – whether he was running or walking?"

I pretended to concede the point, but my brain had raced ahead. *Are you kidding*? Someone – possibly Ellen, although how she was connected with Farini these days I did not know – had persuaded David Morgan to leave his house on some pretext, presumably so that he could set himself up. It reinforced my conviction that I was now hunting a murderer.

I got Mrs Morgan to show me, very roughly, where her son had met his death, and when I left later I retraced his route in the car. He had been struck at the crossroads where the North Circular Road carries fast-moving traffic around the perimeter of London, but although I drove there and back several times I could find no clue to where David had been going. It could not have been far, or else he would have taken his car. I thought initially of an assignation, and there were a few public benches on the Common, but that would have entailed a detour. Then I noticed a public telephone on the other side of the junction. Could he have come out to phone someone? But why? I began to think of possible reasons but stopped; it was not vitally important at this stage ... perhaps Farini would tell me ...

The performing arts remind me of an iceberg; the tip representing those who have succeeded; and the vast underwater mass, the overwhelming majority who struggle to survive. In the way that many of these people's lives are divorced from reality, so certain reputations are created from illusion. James Farini was a typical example – a producer and one-time director whose reputation was not borne out by his track record; a rising star in his youth, burned out before his talent could be fulfilled. Fifteen years before, Farini had something of a cult following but a series of disappointing productions should have eroded the legend. He kept the battered remains intact through an instinctive flair for publicity. His production of *Romeo and Juliet*, for example, had featured a genuine 16-year-old Middle European princess in the starring role, and later he had launched the same girl on an international modelling career. No-one quite knew why his later films were so disappointing, but undoubtedly it had something to do with the pressures of trying to keep his foothold on a slippery slope. The greater the pressure, the more he had been inclined to clutch at straws better left alone.

Farini had lived in London for ten years, ostensibly because he claimed to be an ardent anglophile, but more likely because – as Ellen had suggested – he had made too many enemies in the United States. The large, white, detached house not far from the Heath at Hampstead was imposing, if one did not look too closely at the exterior plaster and woodwork, which could not have been painted since he had moved in. Yet somehow it did not seem to matter. The place had character and, coupled with an owner of Farini's larger-than-life personality, the combination projected an ambience which may well have had something to do with his regular appearances in print. Even Farini's entrance might have been lifted from one of his films. Framed in the doorway, and wearing a white suit set off by a black polo-neck jumper, he was holding on to the collar of an evil-looking black Doberman which might have been at my throat but for the very firm restraint.

Farini, presumably through practice, had mastered the trick of greeting a guest like a long-lost brother while at the same time issuing a warning from the side of his mouth not to make any sudden moves until "Nero" had got used to him. I get on quite well with most dogs but I had the feeling Nero did not like me – or anyone apart from his master – but fortunately it gave the impression of being well-trained, sufficient at least to keep his dislike in check.

The dog's belligerence was compensated in part by the warmth of Farini's welcome; one of such sincerity that I began to wonder if we had met on some previous occasion. As a matter of fact, his face and general bearing was faintly familiar, but I put that down to the fact that I had seen his photograph on numerous occasions in the newspapers.

The house was on three floors but looked larger because of the height of the ceilings. The living-quarters on the ground level were approached by about a dozen stone steps and I was told that the basement slightly below road level, and reached through a separate entrance, had been turned into a gymnasium and games room.

Farini told me he lived on his own for most of the time, although he entertained occasionally – bringing in sundry girlfriends for the occasion, "paid" by being invited to share his bed for the night. "I'm never lonely," he assured me. "I *prefer* to be on my own."

"Yet you have had two wives and at least three live-in mistresses," I pointed out, playing the earnest feature writer.

"Exactly. Doesn't that prove my point?" he asked with a disarming chuckle.

I studied him dispassionately. He was an impressive-looking man; several inches shorter than me but stockily built and possessing a restless energy. Judging from the neck muscles that could not be concealed by the high-necked jumper, and the way he carried himself it was apparent – at least, to me – that he made full use of his gymnasium, although obviously not to extremes. From his high colour and slight fleshiness around the jaw line I guessed he was probably a connoisseur of food and drink, and the exercise may well have been his excuse for not counting the calories. For all that he had a charismatic manner, and several times in the early part of our "interview" I had to remind myself that I had come to bury Farini, not praise him.

After showing me over the house, dropping several hints that he would make himself available if the paper wanted to take a few photographs, we adjourned to his study, or what he preferred to call his "creative zone". I could see what he was getting at, although how much of it was affectation it was impossible to guess. My initial reaction was that it was more like an aquarium than a study. There were two windows but the curtains were kept drawn so that the room was in perpetual shade, with spotlights in the ceiling picking up whatever feature he considered necessary for his inspiration of the moment. There were four large, heated tanks of tropical fish resting on chest-high fitted bookcases on each side of the room; on top of a cupboard at one end was another tank, without water, which seemed to be empty until some time later I thought I detected a movement and realised it housed a couple of snakes.

I expressed surprise at the hot-house decor. "I've heard of tropical fish being used as a therapy for mentally disturbed patients – it's obvious they can have a soothing effect, but I wouldn't have thought a *creative* influence ... "

"Film is a very visual medium," he explained,

pleased to have intrigued me. "It has a lot to do with images ... a hangover from my happy days as a director."

I watched the fish for a few seconds, looking from tank to tank and beginning to see what he was getting at. "What about the snakes?"

He walked over to the tank, picked up one of the snakes and held it up for inspection; it was about four feet long. "They just interest me. This character and his friend are boa constrictors."

"The only time I've seen a boa constrictor was in a comic strip. It was a huge, thick creature coiled round the hero, about the crush him to death."

He put the snake back. "It couldn't have been one of mine; they haven't left the house. Besides, they're a bit young for that sort of thing."

"They don't seem to *do* very much ...?"

"I suppose not ... there *isn't* much to do for a snake when you come to think of it ... apart from eat and sleep. Let's see if I can get them to perform for you ..." He left the room for a moment and returned holding a couple of mice by their tails. He put them in with the snakes, but they were ignored. One of the mice trotted over to examine the snakes, sniffing at them with only mild curiosity. I was fascinated by the total absence of fear.

Farini guessed what I was thinking. "People imagine it is cruel to give snakes their food live, but as you can see, the mice are not exactly terrified."

I was more squeamish than him and looked away, pretending to take a renewed interest in the fish. I asked how long he had collected such unusual pets. He did not answer directly. "I don't regard them as pets, of course. If I had my life again I would have been a naturalist ... ideally running a small zoo. In practical terms it would have meant that I had to specialise, and in that case I would have concentrated on tropical fish and reptiles."

I could not be really sure whether he was speaking the truth, or merely trying to provide an interesting angle for my story. I played safe and encouraged him to elaborate. "I could understand specialising in chimps or gorillas, or even dolphins, but never snakes or lizards ... You are not going to say they are highly intelligent ... ?"

He grinned. "What has intelligence got to do with it? Zoologists can spend their lives studying *fleas*. I would find *that* boring, perhaps, but probably only through ignorance. The more you learn, the more you want to learn. It's impossible to encompass everything and I began to narrow my interest a few years ago when I was filming along the Amazon – the most incredible place on earth. Do you realise that man is destroying the rain forests at such a rate that ... " He stopped himself with an apparent effort and apologised. "Once I get on my hobby-horse, you will need to stay the night to finish the interview. Let's talk about films ... "

I had prepared a number of questions calculated to disarm him and, as he supplied the information he thought I wanted, I went through the motions of taking notes. I listened with only half an ear, waiting for the opportunity to link my questions to the subject that interested me far more than Farini's career. However, the interim dialogue served to feed his ego, and he was mellow by the time I got round to what I described as his more recent run of "bad luck".

I did not encounter any significant note of caution until I repeated a rumour that he was having problems financing his latest project. The indulgent expression of good humour that had remained fixed since the start of the interview suddenly vanished, to be replaced a moment or two later by a forced smile.

"Let us be perfectly frank with each other, Matt. I can give you a number of answers to that question, depending on the tone of your article. Obviously you are completely free to write what you like about me within reason, but I must say that since I haven't seen your by-line before, I don't know whether you are going to do a sympathetic piece, a stiletto job, or something in between. I'm not asking for anything cosmetic, but nor do I expect you to highlight *all* my warts ..."

I looked hurt at the suggestion. "I thought I made it clear that I am an admirer of your work."

He looked relieved. "Then perhaps I can speak off the record for a moment?"

I nodded and told him what he wanted to hear – which for different reasons happened to be the truth: "The Chronicle will not print anything that you would find objectionable."

He adopted the expression of someone about to put all his cards on the table. "I'm more than happy to trust in your judgement," he announced. "You have to understand that money is always a sensitive issue to producers. It is true that we have not yet got *all* the finance for the next project, but it is early days yet. I've got several irons in the fire."

"I heard that you had been to the City, but were turned down ... ?"

"Oh? To listen to some people – and there are a lot of jealous people around – you would think I have to go knocking at doors like a vacuum salesman."

" ... One of the medium-size pension funds, Allman & Spinks. Chap named Anthony Longstaff ? "

"The guy who disappeared ... who told you that?" The outburst was so indignant, it was difficult to determine whether he was stalling, or merely furious with the rumour-mongers.

"Their security adviser, David Morgan. Claimed he had a tape of a discussion between you and Longstaff."

"Is that so ... ?"

Now he was definitely playing for time and he continued to hesitate before actually ducking the issue. He got up. "Would you excuse me for just a second, Matt?" he asked, leaving the room without waiting for a response. There was nothing I could do and I sat there fuming with frustration at not being able to follow up my advantage.

I had no idea where Farini had gone, but the tinkle of the telephone bell indicated that he had picked up an extension in another room. It was obvious he had become suspicious and was phoning the Daily Chronicle. For a few moments I was tempted to lift the receiver and listen in, but it would have given me no advantage. Instead, I decided to play it by ear.

I got up and wandered over to the bookcase, idly browsing through the contents. It was a disappointing mixture to me ... a large section of 'popular' fiction, the sort of material he might at one stage have considered adapting for a film, and a rather better-quality section on natural history. The books were arranged neatly under subjects with their spines facing outwards, but occasionally a decorated cover was displayed in full, including several eye-catching dust-jackets. Because of the specialist nature of the collection there were some large-format paperbacks and I was fascinated by a horrific close-up of a fish that seemed to be staring straight at me. It decorated the cover of an American paperback called *The Piranha Book*, and the subtitle read: 'An Account of the ill-famed Piranha fishes of the Rivers of tropical South America'. The photographer had focussed on the terrible teeth which, because of the perspective, reminded me of a shark, although I knew piranhas to be quite tiny ... no bigger than some of the tropical fish in the room. Come to think of it, the species in one of the tanks did bear a resemblance to the illustration, and I went over to take a closer look. Frustratingly they seemed determined to keep their teeth hidden from my view, but it did seem a remarkable coincidence. I had not realised that carnivorous species could be kept in the home, but as far as my untrained eye could detect they looked the same and I was not about to stick my finger in the water to find out.

Farini came back into the room to put an end to my speculation. The charm had gone. "I've just been on to the Chronicle. There is no-one in features answering to your name. What is going on? Who are you?"

"I gave you my real name, but I must admit I don't work for the Chronicle ... "

"And you're not a film writer."

"Sorry."

He seemed exasperated – which was understandable enough – and looked from me to Nero, as though debating whether or not to let him at my throat. With the discovery of the piranhas fresh in my mind I had a crazy notion of diving for the tank and upsetting them over the dog. I could visualize the confusion it would cause, but another quick glance at Nero reminded me that he was not likely to co-operate; nor were the fish likely to be very effective out of water.

However, Farini was not as desperate as I had imagined. "Are you going to tell me why you are here – or do I have to call the police?" he enquired in a business-like manner.

I shrugged. "I used that ploy because I thought it was the only way I could get past the door, but I don't mind telling you the truth. I worked for Anthony Longstaff – buying books for the pension fund ... " I handed him a business card to corroborate the statement, but he barely glanced at it. "After he disappeared Morgan and I put our heads together. He was supposed to come and see you about the meeting you had with Longstaff on the day before he disappeared."

"He may have said he was coming to see me, but he never turned up. I've never met the man."

"Nor will you – he's dead. Killed a week ago in what the police think was a hit-and-run accident. Bit of a coincidence, don't you think?"

"I'm sorry to hear that – as I would about any young person snuffed out before his time."

"How did you know he was young?"

"It's a reasonable assumption that he hadn't turned 65, or he wouldn't still be working for the firm. Anyway, whatever his age, I don't see what it has to do with me ... "

"Let me ask what he intended to ask: What about the meeting with Longstaff? It's important because you may have been the last person to see him alive."

"Why? Is there any suggestion that he is also dead? Either way, I am not prepared to talk to strangers about matters that are private ... that is, of concern only to Longstaff and myself."

"No need to be coy," I pointed out, irritably. "I

heard Morgan's tape."

"What tape?"

"It seems Longstaff was in the habit of keeping a verbatim record of all his business dealings."

"You mean, secretly?"

"Without the other person's knowledge, if that is what you mean."

"And where is that tape now?"

I shrugged. "I'm not sure whether legally it would be classified as the property of Allman & Spinks, or of Longstaff – or his estate. I shouldn't worry – no-one is going to do anything with it ... unless the police decide you've got something to hide. What time did you leave Longstaff?"

"You forfeited the right to an answer the moment you tricked your way past that door."

"You would rather talk to the police?"

"If necessary. I have nothing to hide; when we parted Longstaff was in excellent spirits. Now ... I think *you* have overstayed your welcome, Mr Coll. If you don't leave at once, Nero might be induced to speed you on your way."

I felt humiliated, not only at the way I had bungled the interview, but by the way I was being kicked out with my tail between my legs. I had learned nothing; only succeeded in putting Farini on his guard. My initial anger was replaced by a sense of personal shame. I still had the option of going to the police, making out sufficient of a case to convince Murdoch, at least, that there were grounds for a proper investigation. Yet there was something underhand, almost sneaky, about being an informer. I believed that any man of integrity should put up, or shut up. Besides, I owed it to David Morgan to settle the score with Farini. I showed myself out.

Nine

There is a surprisingly fine line between planning ahead and worrying oneself sick; and on returning to Ardley I was feeling very low. That may seem strange to those who know me and do not regard me as the worrying kind. I am not, of course; not in the sense that I waste time brooding over something that may never happen, but my impotence at Farini's guilt rankled. I was determined not to let him get away with it and I did not want to be unprepared for our next meeting.

In any case, I had to clear the decks and start afresh. What I needed to recharge my batteries was work entirely unrelated to the Longstaff business and this I was able to find in the shop in abundance. Even what was normally regarded as spare time was occupied with work on my next catalogue, a mammoth undertaking. The aim was to be so tired at bed-time that I would collapse into an exhausted sleep that had no room for the troubled ghost of David Morgan – or Farini, with whom my future was irrevocably linked. I followed this pattern for three days with satisfactory results – not only in terms of progress achieved, but in clearing my head of discordant memories. Then my conviction about not brooding in anticipation was vindicated – in the form of a totally unexpected phone call from James Farini.

It is equally true that I was unprepared for another confrontation so quickly, but any planning on my part would have been geared to trying to get at Farini; I could not have anticipated his volunteering to meet me. Of course, with good reason to be suspicious of his motives I took the precaution of assuming I had to be doubly careful, but, prepared or not, it seemed too good an opportunity to miss. Without denigrating David Morgan, he was by his own admission inexperienced in this sort of situation; I was not. I also knew that by walking into what could be a trap with my eyes open, I was consciously reducing the odds. With any luck, it would be a question of pitting my wits against those of Farini, who, having taken the initiative, might be somewhat over-confident.

Farini's story was that he had been reflecting on what he now realised was an unnecessarily defensive reaction during our meeting ... that he was invariably inclined to be over-sensitive over money matters ... and that finding my business card later when he changed jackets prompted him to decide it was time to grasp the nettle – provided I gave an undertaking that anything he was prepared to reveal about the meeting with Longstaff remained a secret between us. He said nothing about David Morgan, presumably sticking to his original claim that he had never met him, and I did not want to rock the boat. I agreed to his conditions without hesitation; equally without sincerity. If what he was going to tell me was the truth and my suspicions were to prove unfounded then I would keep my word. If he lied, I would automatically be released from that promise.

As a matter of principle I went through the motions of suggesting a meeting on 'neutral' territory, but did not argue when he insisted on privacy. To give him credit, he also made it clear he did not much care where we met so long as our discussion could not be overheard. I appeared to match his mood of indifference and concluded that since the meeting was his idea I would be content to fall in with his proposal.

He kept up the act. "I suppose we could meet in Hyde Park – fourth bench behind the bushes by the lake – or something like that? That's what the spies do in my films. Trouble is, it's a bit chilly at this time of year. Why don't we be civilised and have a drink at my place?"

"Suits me."

We settled for an evening appointment so that I need not neglect the shop during the day – and then spend the night with Laura ... what was left of it after the police had finished listening to the confession I would have dragged out of him by then. I phoned Laura and told her to expect me during the evening, but not tying myself down to a precise time, and then sat down to plan my tack.

I was determined not to let him off the hook this time, preparing my questions with the thoroughness of a lawyer. I tried to anticipate every possible answer – unexpected, as well as those that were obvious. I was not tied by the decorum of the courtroom, which meant that I was not concerned with proving anything "beyond a shadow of doubt"; nor was I too proud – should he prove more intelligent than me – to throw the brief overboard and resort to violence. I could at least be sure that Farini did not have my training in dirty tricks. The police, like lawyers, might have to adhere to a code of ethics, but I did not much care whether the confession was volunteered or obtained under duress. In what I considered was a good cause I would have no compunction. The only problem was his dog. I would have to think of a way of incapacitating Nero, if the need arose.

In the event, when Farini greeted me at the front

door his openness and charm made my preconceived ideas of violence seem unnecessarily crude. Even Nero appeared to have been carefully briefed – or had undergone a personality transplant. But although the atmosphere was totally disarming my suspicion was too far ingrained to allow me to relax. *Nothing has changed*, I assured myself. *For all your blue eyes and dimples, you're as guilty as sin*. Nevertheless, I had to wait for Farini to make the first move.

He said nothing about Longstaff until I was seated, and then, for dramatic effect, perhaps – he produced a script and casually dropped it in my lap. "The *reason* for my meeting with Anthony Longstaff ... no doubt you have read the book?"

I glanced at the title-page and shook my head. "Forgive my ignorance, but I can never find time to keep up with the current bestsellers. There are around 40,000 books published here every year, and that constitutes only the tip of the iceberg."

"But you've heard of it?"

"I read the reviews, of course. Seems to be a talented writer."

He laughed. "The understatement of the year! Perhaps I'm biased ... " He broke off to fetch a bottle of malt whisky, three quarters full, from a cocktail cabinet. He showed me the label with an expression approaching reverence. "Have you read the reviews of *this*?"

I shook my head. "Another bestseller?"

"Heaven forbid!" He seemed shocked. "Hardly – at this price ... *three* times the cost of most malt whiskies. However, I assure you it is worth every cent ... I don't give it to anyone, so consider yourself privileged ... "

"Thanks, I do."

He produced some glasses and poured me a

generous measure, but when he did not take any for himself I was instantly on the alert. I would not have put it past him to drug the whisky.

I prepared to call his bluff by asking why he was not joining me. He returned to the cocktail cabinet and plaintively held up a bottle of tonic water. "Not from choice. It's doctor's orders," he replied, pulling a face. "Damned ulcer, I'm afraid."

I winked. "If we listened to doctors, we would cut out food and drink altogether. Practically everything we buy is harmful in one way or another. I believe in moderation ... one drink can't do any harm, unless you're an alcoholic."

"You mean like on special occasions?" he asked, beginning to look interested.

I nodded.

" ... Besides which you are one of these people who simply can't drink alone?"

"Sure am," I declared, completing the conspiracy.

He grinned. "That's good enough for me." He poured himself the equivalent of a 'double' of the malt. "I've always been a bit low on will-power," he added with a grin.

I began to have second thoughts over my initial reaction. Because I had been suspicious from the outset, it seemed that I had over-reacted and there was still a possibility that I was barking up the wrong tree. "They knew better in the Middle Ages, when there was always an official 'taster' on hand to test for poison in the food or drink." Suddenly embarrassed, I removed his glass and poured the contents into mine. "I'm not being greedy, but I don't want your ulcer on my conscience. Stick to tonic water. One of these days you can make up for it."

He laughed sheepishly and did as he was instructed

even to the extent of getting a clean glass. When full of tonic water he raised it in salute: "Success!"

"Success!" I echoed, sipping at my whisky to savour it. The texture was as smooth as I had anticipated, but the alcohol was strong enough to shrivel my tongue. I put it down to the fact that I usually took my whisky with water or ice, but it would have been sacrilege to have diluted such a fine malt. In any case, whisky – any brand – should not be sipped like a liqueur. I swallowed a mouthful, and it was not until the liquid reached my stomach that I really appreciated its quality. My tongue no longer burned; everything seemed pleasantly warm, and I was soon feeling a little light-headed. I wondered what he had paid for the bottle, whether it was worth it – at whatever price – or whether the label was largely affectation or to do with snob appeal. The malt was certainly smooth. Without thinking I took another drop, and another. I was beginning to see what he was getting at; it was remarkable stuff.

Farini had begun to tell me about the film and his early thoughts on casting. Since I had already heard the tape covering the same ground, it was of little interest, and I began to wonder why he did not come to the point.

I was already feeling slightly inebriated, but knew the idea was ridiculous. It reminded me of Laura who always complained that even a half glass of wine caused her senses to swim – which, as I always pointed out, could only be psychological. Yet here was I, old loudmouth, experiencing similar symptoms. Admittedly malt whisky was considerably more intoxicating than wine, but I was hardly a newcomer to spirits.

It was probably at this point that I realised my

instincts had been correct, and that I had fallen for his double-bluff with the ulcer. I felt dejected as well as dizzy; Farini was still outsmarting me every step of the way; if I had drunk any faster I might have been unconscious by now.

He droned on – not yet suspecting that I was on to him – about his plans for the film and I was able to concentrate on a course of action. If I was to 'accidentally' spill my drink he would insist on replenishing it. The logical alternative was to declare that I did not like the brand and politely decline to finish it – which would bring us back to the *status quo*. Providing I had not already absorbed too much of the drug, that was probably the safest bet.

On the other hand, I was intrigued by what Farini intended to do when I lost consciousness; it would be much more exciting to go along with his plan and turn the tables when he was off-guard. Then it occurred to me that I was making an assumption that he was drugging me; that, in fact, there might be poison in the whisky – and that resolved my indecision.

To continue the subterfuge I took another sip through closed lips, and then asked if I could use the bathroom. "I meant to ask when I arrived, but you shoved this delightful drink in my hand. I always want to go after a long journey ... in fact, as soon as I get in the car if I know there are no public toilets en route ..."

He laughed sympathetically and gestured with his forefinger. "Second door on the left ... "

I got up, not bothering to conceal my unsteadiness but saying nothing, and went out. Then, praying that the sound would not carry, I put two fingers down my throat and vomited into the lavatory bowl. There can be few experiences more unpleasant and exhausting than induced sickness, but stoically I repeated the process until I was sure there was nothing of any significance left in my stomach. Afterwards I washed my mouth out with cold water from the tap and finally drank as much of it as I could.

When I left the bathroom I still felt shaky but psychologically a lot better. Returning to Farini's 'creative zone' I justified the time taken by claiming that I had suddenly felt very tired and had felt the need to splash some cold water on my face.

He waved a deprecating hand and suggested that the journey had probably taken more out of me than I had thought. "I never drive more than a hundred miles at a stretch," he said. "Must have taken three hours, surely?"

I nodded. "Probably. Anyway, I'm feeling better now. You were talking about the film ... ? Sounds exciting. I wish *I* had some cash to invest ... "

He smiled dutifully. "I might take you up on that one of these days ... "

"But you hinted that it hadn't been easy – so you went to see Longstaff? Was that anything to do with the family connection?"

"Something like that. Obviously I keep my ears to the ground, so I knew he was not as reactionary as most of those guys. I also heard he can be difficult to reach, so I thought he might be amused by the fact we had married the same woman."

"And was he?"

Farini grinned. "He's only human. I had also heard rumours that he was human in other ways too – that he might be interested in some of the beautiful ladies I've got lined up for the film."

My head was still slightly woozy and I made no effort to conceal a yawn. For his benefit I lifted the glass of whisky to my lips and pretended to sip from it.

Even as I was wondering how to get rid of the remaining drink, my luck changed for the better. The phone rang and Farini got up to answer it. When he knew who the caller was, he decided to take it in the other room. Although I was tempted to eavesdrop, my priority was to get rid of the drugged liquor. While he was in the room my options had been limited, but with greater scope I decided to pour the drink into the fish-tanks. I endeavoured to spread it evenly in the hope that the water would dilute sufficiently to render it virtually harmless. I was not concerned about killing the fish, but did not want anything dramatic to happen too quickly to distract Farini.

When he returned I was pouring more whisky from the bottle into my glass. I looked up, almost apologetically. "I hope you don't mind me helping myself ... ?"

I could not have said anything better. "On the contrary, Matt. It's good to see someone appreciate its qualities ... "

He apologised in turn for the interruption and asked me to refresh his memory. It did not seem feasible that a single telephone call would cause a blank in his memory so I concluded he was testing me. I adopted a look of intense concentration for several seconds and then made a stab at snapping my fingers. "You were talking about your film ..!" When he nodded encouragingly I continued with a note of triumph: "... You were talking about the film. You went to see Longstaff ... because ... because you knew his wife .. or rather, you married his wife. Sorry! He married *your* wife ... Is that right?"

Perhaps I overdid the note of confusion, but I wanted to get a reaction from Farini. I knew that *I* would have been quite irritated with anyone who had clearly not been listening properly – especially if he had just helped himself to more whisky without appearing to realise he was already slightly inebriated. Yet Farini not only remained expressionless, but gave himself away by starting to go over the same ground again. He was obviously playing for time, waiting for the drug to take over, so I decided to encourage him. I yawned widely and leaned my head back against the armchair, closing my eyes. "Please carry on," I announced. "I am listening, just resting my eyes. It helps me concentrate sometimes. I think I've been straining my eyes recently ... one of the drawbacks to my work ... "

He had been given another chance to react innocently, to offer sympathy, a cold compress; even willingness to continue the conversation later. But he did not seem to hear or care what I was saying, and his indifference cleared away any lingering vestige of doubt in my mind.

Instead, he began to outline the screenplay again, his voice no longer animated but droning on one level. I wondered what effect the drug was supposed to have, apart from drowsiness. Perhaps he was trying to hypnotise me. I decided to play it by ear and started to breathe more evenly and deeply until at length he stopped speaking. I resisted the temptation to open my eyes and after a few minutes I sensed him move across to me. I felt his breath on my face as he whispered my name.

Lazily I opened drugged eyes and saw him only a few inches away, studying me carefully. " ... Very interesting," I slurred, as though I had not missed a word. "Good film ... "

I half closed my eyes again and watched him return to his seat, satisfied that everything was going to plan.

He waited another few seconds while I pretended to doze off again and then addressed me in a friendly, more relaxed voice. "Matt ... Are you listening?"

I took a deep breath as though trying to pull myself together. " ... 'Cos I'm listening ... jus ... t ... restin' my eyes ... "

"You wanted to know about my meeting with Longstaff. I haven't finished yet."

" ... His wife ... *your* wife ... "

"No. About the money ... He wouldn't give me the money ... "

I made a show of desperately trying to open my eyes, and failing. "I know ... on the tape ... "

"What did the tape *say* ... ?"

"Just restin' m'eyes ... "

His voice retained its warmth and friendliness but there was now a note of urgency about it. "Matt, pay attention – it's important! What did we say on the tape?"

I assumed from his tone that I was supposed to be able to answer, and presumably speak the truth, but since the tape had run out prematurely I did not know what had transpired beyond the cut-off point. I decided to stall. " ... No money ... "

I was conscious of Farini leaning over me again. "What did he *sound* like?"

The part that Morgan and I had heard sounded normal enough but Farini must have had a reason for asking. I played an inspired hunch. "... Tired ..." I let him place whatever interpretation he liked on the word, which might just as easily have been a reference to my own state.

But Farini took the bait. "Tired, was he? What about the jacuzzi?"

I had no idea what he was talking about, but

vaguely echoed the word "Jacuzzi ..."

"Blast!"

What I said had obviously struck home, but I have no idea what significance the jacuzzi could possibly have. Had Longstaff been drowned? It seemed unlikely; what would Farini have done with the body? Frustratingly I did not get a chance to pursue that channel of enquiry because Farini returned to his obvious concern about the tape and what it might reveal. "Did Morgan make any copies?"

Searching for inspiration, I evaded the question by pretending to lose consciousness. I allowed my head to slump forward on to my chest, and a hand to drop off my lap and hang suspended, a few inches from the ground. A moment later I was suffering for my deviousness because Farini slapped me across the face several times in an effort to wake me up. I maintained the act for several seconds before allowing my better judgement to take over. I forced my eyes open and asked where I was.

Farini ignored the plea and repeated the question. "I must know about the tape," he insisted. "Did Morgan make any copies? Did he play it to anyone else?"

I made a stab at shaking my head while simulating the continued lack of co-ordination.

"Are you sure?" he demanded.

I realised that although I had the temporary advantage of being able to think clearly, while he was off-guard, imagining me to be drugged, I was not *using* my brains, and therefore getting nowhere. Somehow I had to outflank him and this would be doubly difficult while I was restricted to monosyllabilic responses to his questions. Presumably something had happened at Longlands that might incriminate him if it was captured on tape; and presumably it had something to do with Longstaff being drugged. The $64 question was: what had happened to him then?

It occurred to me at that point that if the same was in store for me I would be finding out soon enough – by which time it would probably be too late. Meanwhile I knew I was in for another stinging slap across the face if I did not answer his last question pretty quickly. Morgan had *not* made copies, of course, but I could not decide whether or not to admit this. If Farini believed there was only one he would probably feel justified in killing the only surviving person to have listened to it; if he thought it had been heard by several Allman & Spinks executives he might have less incentive to kill me, as just one of several 'witnesses', but equally he might panic and leave the country. Such is my ego that I decided I could control the situation better if he continued to focus his attention on me. "Jus..h Morg'n an' me," I slurred.

I could sense that Farini was almost satisfied, but the stakes were too high for him to leave any stone unturned. His next question may have seemed logical, but was even more difficult to answer. "What happened to Longstaff?"

I took a chance, hoping that if it was not the answer he expected, it would be attributed to the fantasies of a drugged mind. "D...dead," I pronounced with an effort, trying not to overact.

I waited with bated breath for a reaction but he said nothing, and I knew that Longstaff was indeed dead.

Farini did not let up. "We know he's dead ... but what *happened* to him?"

I had no idea what he was talking about, and stalled. "D...drugg...ed."

"*After* that ... ?" Farini urged.

"J'cuzzi," I mumbled, taking a stab in the dark, sensing I was on the right track.

"*Then* what?"

I was beginning to panic. Something had happened in the jacuzzi. I had already speculated about Farini drowning him, but had found no answer to what he might have done with Longstaff's body. Perhaps he had buried it somewhere in the grounds – it was a vast place ... but somehow that seemed too *ordinary* for a flamboyant personality. *How to get rid of the body? Dissolve it in acid, perhaps.* I recalled Haigh, the acid-bath murderer, and went off the idea. A bath was one thing, but the jacuzzi was enormous. My mind kept coming back to the problem of disposing of a body.

Perhaps he cut it up and fed it to Nero?. The idea, horrific though it seemed, was more amusing than realistic, but it set up a train of thought that recalled the American magazine about piranhas. Piranhas!? Tropical man-eating fish would be in their element in the warm water of the jacuzzi! I imagined the technical problems would have been awesome, but not beyond someone of Farini's imagination and ingenuity, particularly in view of his knowledge of tropical fish. I had nothing to lose by speculation. If I was wrong, there was always my drugged, incoherent mind to fall back on. Struggling to control my excitement I waited until he assumed I had fallen asleep again. When he shook me violently, I hammed it up like mad, forcing my eyes open and staring unseeingly at him until the sight of his face triggered off a memory. "J'cuzzi ... " I repeated vacantly.

He grabbed me by the jaw, pressing his thumb and forefinger into my cheeks. The grip was quite painful but I did not react until he commanded: 'Stay awake, I said! What *happened* in the jacuzzi?"

I endeavoured to look as though I was struggling to remember through the fog of confusion. "F...fish..."

The satisfaction of seeing him draw in his breath was overwhelming. It was a stab in the dark, but apparently an accurate one. Frustratingly, when he released my jaw I had to maintain the act and let my head fall forward so I could no longer see his expression, but I could sense that he was unnerved. He got up and began pacing the room, until he remembered my presence and presumably pulled himself together. At least, when he came over and commanded me to go back to sleep, the voice was controlled and even gentle. Finally satisfied with my condition, he moved over to the telephone and dialled a number – which from the number of digits, I guessed was a local call.

Under control again, his voice was relaxed and remarkably cool as he announced himself. "It's me," he began, not identifying himself in any other way, or the person to whom he was speaking. "We *will* need that tape, after all. I'll explain later ... yes ... yes, he's still here. Had a bit too much to drink, but I'll run him home later ..."

For a split second, as he stopped to listen to the person at the other end, I was disconcerted. *Take me home*!? But logic warned me that he was probably being cautious on the phone; that the only justification for undertaking a three-hour car journey at this time of night was to be over a hundred miles away from Hampstead when he disposed of my body. I doubted whether he even knew where I lived.

I forced myself to stop speculating and caught the rest of his conversation. "Are you sure you have double-checked? Good. I'll take his car, so you'll have to bring me back. You know where to go? ... Good ...

No, not outside. Keep out of sight. I'll find *you*. Right, we're leaving now."

I had my eyes closed all the time, but when he put the phone down I sensed him watching me, and I was relieved that my head was slumped forward so that he could not examine my face too closely. Fortunately he had seen the drug work on Longstaff, so at no stage had he felt the need to double-check I was not conscious. Even so, I was aware of my heart beginning to pound with anxiety.

However, Farini was satisfied and a few seconds later I heard him leave the room. Tentatively I opened my eyes and met the baleful stare of Nero, apparently content to trust in his master's infallibility, yet watchful nevertheless. I doubted if he would remain inactive if I attempted to surprise Farini now. It was that awareness more than anything else that prompted me to wait for a better opportunity to turn the tables, supporting my instinct from the outset – to wait and see what would transpire. Well, much had already transpired, but although there was now no doubt at all of Farini's guilt I had no evidence that would stand up in a court of law. If I was to overpower Farini at this point and call the police, what could I tell them that he would not instantly deny?

On the other hand, there was still time for him to put a foot wrong, and if I could now catch him out in a further criminal act, they would have to listen to the rest of the story. My imagination started playing tricks and I had visions of him driving me to the scene of an earlier crime – to Longlands – to the jacuzzi full of piranhas ... I saw the half eaten corpse of Longstaff rising out of the water ... Farini, terrified, turning to run and tripping over my outstretched leg ... into the water. I wondered how long I would wait before dialling 999.

I closed my eyes when I heard Farini returning and, as he searched through my trousers and jacket pockets for my car keys, I realised he had put on a pair of leather driving-gloves. Then, with the keys in his own pocket, he squatted on the floor in front of my chair and arranged me over his shoulder in a fireman's lift. Taking a few deep breaths, he stood up quite smoothly – exhaling theatrically with the effort but obviously finding my dead weight within his capabilities as he carried me out. Able to open my eyes again I felt a little more confident. Nero had got up to follow us, his eyes never leaving mine, but on Farini's command to 'stay' he stopped in his tracks.

Sight in these circumstances can be a double-edged sword. A dead-weight is strength-sapping and, as Farini began to tire and his legs falter, the last part of the journey – down the stone steps at the front of the house, and along the gravel drive – provided some anxious moments for me – expecting at any moment to be dropped on my head. Luckily my fears were misplaced and I arrived at the Citroen in one piece, although Farini was sweating and out of breath. He crouched to stand me on my feet again and then leant me back against the car. I was not sure whether my legs were supposed to give way, but I calculated from the way my body was spreadeagled against the car that it would support me well enough if I kept my knees reasonably stiff. When the door had been unlocked he more or less stuffed me into the back, banging my head against the roof in the process. The pain was quite sharp but I stifled a groan and ended up being bundled inside with my head touching the floor and feet up on the seat.

No-one could realise how disorientating the position

was when the car moved off and I tried to see where we were going. All I could make out in the dark was the occasional street lamp. At the outset I could tell from the gear-shifts that we were going uphill, which indicated we were heading north – in the opposite direction from Ardley – but then I quickly lost my bearings. Road signs and even the names of shops were below the angle of my vision and I did not dare risk propping myself up. To pass the time I day-dreamed about jumping Farini the next time he stopped at traffic lights, wrapping my fingers round his throat, imagining his panic reaction at the shock. I resisted the temptation because I knew the satisfaction would be immense but shortlived when we were so near to uncovering the next phase of his plan.

Within fifteen minutes the ordeal was over. The Citroen came to a stop and Farini got out and opened the rear door. He tried to get me up on the back seat, but finding my inert body too cumbersome, he looked round to make sure we were not overlooked, then took my feet and unceremoniously pulled me out. Fortunately he stopped before my shoulders or head hit the pavement and then sat me up so that he could get me into the fireman's lift again.

So near and yet so far, it was frustrating not to know where we were, but I dared not open my eyes until I was over his shoulder and from that angle one pavement looks like any other. He needed only three or four strides to reach the bell and I was on tenterhooks, my adrenalin surfing through me like a giant wave of excitement. I was conscious of a light being switched on and of the front door opening and making a rattling noise as though it was hollow, more like a shop door. We were greeted by a familiar voice demanding: "Who are you?" The tone was agressively in character. It was Stephen Gorton.

I felt Farini brush past him. "You were told to expect me ... " he announced authoritatively. "Do you mind turning off that light. We can't stay here in full view with this on my back."

Recognising me at last Gorton demanded to know what I was doing there: then, recovering his wits, he asked: "Wait a minute ... what's going on anyway? I had a phone call about someone coming over with some books. She said I would know you; I don't. The only person I know is him – he's a bookseller called Matthew Coll. What happened to him?"

Farini ignored him and carried me through into the work area, out of view of the shop window. Without a word he lowered his shoulder and let me fall. Sudden though the move was, I might have braced myself, but not knowing whether he was watching I simply had to relax and trust to luck. Fortunately the distance between my head and shoulders and the floorboards was less than three feet and by opening my eyes just before the impact I was able to tuck my head in and roll over, more like a wheel than the sack of potatoes I felt like.

Presumably Farini did not give me a second glance because he turned to deal with Gorton who had followed us in, spluttering with indignation. "You don't have to worry about Mr Coll," Farini began, by way of explanation. "He's just had too much to drink ..."

"Why have you brought him here?" Gorton demanded.

"Because I thought it was in your best interests."

"What does that mean? Who are you, anyway?"

From the sound of his voice, I had gathered that Farini had his back to me, and cautiously I opened my eyes. Gorton was staring at the American. He was no fool and I was interested to see how he would handle the situation.

Farini chuckled. "Names are not important; let's concentrate on *issues.* You don't know me, of course, but we have a mutual friend ..."

"Oh?" Gorton responded cautiously. "I doubt if we mix in the same circles."

Farini shrugged indifferently. "Please yourself."

"*Business* friend?" speculated Gorton.

"The common factor is our friend here," Farini said, nodding in my direction.

"Anthony Longstaff?! He *is* alive then?"

"Don't lose any sleep over Tony. *This* is the guy you have to worry about – your fellow bookseller."

"Why is that?"

"I'm sure you can guess. Friend Coll has been shooting his mouth off about the deal you had with our mutual friend. He boasted he was going to put the screws on you."

"Screws?"

"He was going to blackmail you ... threaten to go to the police unless you made a substantial contribution to his own *personal* pension fund."

I closed my eyes just in time and was conscious of Gorton staring at me. I heard him curse me under his breath and could feel the waves of hatred as though they had some physical substance.

"There is only one way to deal with blackmailers," persisted Farini. "I don't have to tell you what that is ..."

Gorton cleared his throat nervously. "That's easier said than done. I don't think I could kill a man in cold blood."

"That won't be necessary ... play your cards right

and it will be in self-defence," Farini explained. "He'll be coming round any minute and when he does he will be in a foul mood. He's already told me he wanted to humiliate you, and knowing him that probably means physically too. All I'm suggesting is that forewarned is forearmed ..."

"What does that mean?"

" ... that you are *ready* for him! You've got some wicked-looking knives in here ... for cutting leather ..."

"That's still murder," Gorton insisted. "I'm no angel but I couldn't actually set out to kill someone."

"Not even in self-defence?"

Gorton's laugh was mirthless. "Self-defence?!"

I opened my eyes at the sound of Farini moving and watched him take a curve-bladed knife from Gorton's work bench. He held it up questioningly and, when the book-seller shook his head, Farini shrugged. "Pity. There have to be signs of a fight ... " Without warning he took a step forward and rammed the knife into Gorton's midriff. I flinched instinctively in time with the look of horror on the stricken man's face, but even if I was too late to save him I knew I was next on Farini's death list unless I got him first.

As he took his hand off the knife handle, making no effort to withdraw the blade from Gorton's flesh, I was on my feet and at him. Part of my time on the floor had been spent thinking of the most painful way to immobilise him, but I was now conscious of the knife still inches away from his hand. If he pulled it out quickly the curved tip would have the ripping effect of a bayonet and the chances are that Gorton would very quickly bleed to death, so I cut out the frills. Presented with his back, I hit him with clenched fists over both kidneys. The timing was immaculate and I had the satisfaction of hearing him scream with pain.

Gorton had slumped to the ground, fortunately falling on to his side. He was in a bad way, but Farini had to be my priority; I could not afford to take any chances. His legs were beginning to sag but he was fully conscious when I pulled him round by his hair to make sure he could see me. Then clinically I brought my knee up sharply under his testicles. I did it twice. His brief look of surprise was overwhelmed by the fresh tides of pain and I let him fall, knowing he would not move for some time.

Gorton had fainted and he was breathing with difficulty. There was not much blood coming from the wound, but I imagined there would have been interior bleeding, whether or not the blade had penetrated any of the organs. His face had a deathly pallor, but I did not know what to do for him, other than call an ambulance. I was halfway to the phone until I remembered there was still Farini to think about. He had intended to murder both of us, making it appear that we had killed each other in a fight; presumably he would have left some 'evidence' pointing to a motive for the confrontation.

The irony of the situation was not lost on me. If Gorton died there would be no independent witness. It would, however, be rough justice if the police were to find Gorton with Farini's fingerprints on the knife handle.

My mind made up, I removed Farini's gloves and stuffed them in his jacket pocket. Then I dragged him over to Gorton and wrapped the fingers of his right hand round the knife, desperately trying not to disturb the wound. Farini was conscious but too weak to offer any resistance. Then I dialled 999 and asked for the police, adopting the role of an anxious householder disturbed late at night by intruders. I spoke in a hoarse whisper that would also make it difficult to identify the voice. The operator was suitably sympathetic and reacted intelligently until she said that she would have to phone back to ensure that my call was not a hoax. I had nothing to fear but endeavouring to stay in character I pointed out with some agitation that the bell would disturb the intruder, who might then either escape, or even panic and attack me. My point was taken and she promised to send a squad car.

I felt a pang of conscience as I took another look at Gorton. By calling an ambulance first, the few minutes' difference might be enough to save his life, but I suspected he was already too far gone. If by any chance he did survive, he was too devious a person to tell the police the truth. He would probably plead loss of memory until he had been reminded of the 999 call, and he would then no doubt plump for the story of the intruder.

Farini would certainly remain silent, even if he was arrested for attempted murder or causing grievous bodily harm. I looked at him again. He was not unconscious but his face was almost as grey as that of Gorton, and I doubted if he was capable of moving, let alone getting out of the shop, for another fifteen minutes, which in theory gave the police twelve minutes' grace. It seemed to have worked out rather well.

Ten

Despite my uneasiness over Gorton's fate I could not help feeling elated at the turn of events. It was as much as I could do not to hang about until the police arrived to deliver the *coup de grâce*. There was also the nagging awareness that Farini's accomplice was parked somewhere in the vicinity, near enough to be found if I was prepared to delay my departure. However, my car keys left in the ignition served as a reminder to get my priorities right, and when I eventually drove off it was without a backward glance.

I headed for Laura's flat, just behind Marble Arch, reviewing the events of the past few hours. Against my better judgement I had taken a deliberate decision to leave the shop door slightly ajar. It would have seemed less suspicious closed, of course, but with Gorton possibly bleeding to death I did not want the police to waste time ringing the bell or debating whether or not to break in.

My thoughts returned to Farini's partner in crime. While I dislike jumping to conclusions, there was little doubt now that it had been Ellen Longstaff. Gorton had referred to a phone call from a woman and, although David Morgan was the only person who knew about my meeting with the bookseller, it seemed he had no secrets from Ellen. There was also the mysterious phone call that had lured him to his death and I could think of no-one else for whom he would have left his house at that time of night.

Farini had told her to keep out of sight which meant she was unlikely to have seen the police arrive, but presumably there would have been a limit to her patience – after which she would surely have gone to look for him. Alternatively she might have been alerted by the police siren – or the ambulance. Had she gone to investigate she might have seen Farini being detained and she would have needed to be a pretty cool customer not to have driven off in a panic …

I toyed with the idea of driving to Kensington to await her return, in the hope of catching her off-balance, but I was exhausted. The ordeal of the past few hours had taken its toll and I did not feel up to another confrontation. In any case, a sleepless night might soften her up; and it was no more than she deserved.

It was midnight by the time I got to Laura's flat, and she was preparing for bed. She had showered and smelt of talc and a heady perfume I suspected she had put on for my benefit. She was so bewitching that in my normal frame of mind I might have forgotten I was a gentleman and made love to her there and then in the hallway. In the event, I was so tired and preoccupied that I gave her little more than a brotherly peck on the lips and brushed past her into the kitchen.

Anticipating my unflattering order of priorities she recovered her composure and put the kettle on for a pot of tea, while I slumped wearily into a chair by the kitchen table. Glancing at me over her shoulder as she reached for cups and saucers, she remarked; "At least no-one can accuse you of being predictable."

"Come again?" I asked, not yet on the same wavelength.

"Well, having waited up for you, I expected to be carried off to bed – protesting that you only want me for one thing. You do, of course, except that these days it's only because the *cafes* are closed at this time of night."

I got up, suddenly giddy and swaying with fatigue, and put my arms round her affectionately. "My mother warned me about insatiable women ... that it was an experience to look forward to ... second only to a cup of tea ... "

She wriggled free to unplug the kettle. "God, you're so romantic!"

"You know what they say about the English and tea ... ?"

"And stiff upper lips ... ?"

"Stiff what?"

"Exactly! Our relationship must be unique. You remind me of the man who goes up the road for a loaf of bread and doesn't come back for ten years ... "

"Saying that the baker's was closed?"

"It *was* you all the time?"

"Ten years? Seems more like a couple of days," I insisted. "Besides, I did explain that I was caught up in the Longstaff business ... "

"No news yet?" she queried, serious again. "I feel responsible for the mess you are in."

I kissed her on the lips, more warmly. "There *was* no mess until I started one. When I've had some sleep I'll fill you in on the rest of the story to date ... "

"Don't tell me Tony was murdered by his missus for the insurance?" she speculated.

I raised an eyebrow to acknowledge her perception. "That's probably as near to the truth that we'll get. Meanwhile, someone else is making the running;

someone who tonight did his best to kill me – and probably succeeded with Stephen Gorton."

Laura had learned not to fuss over me, but although her expression did not change it was not difficult to detect the change in her attitude – the concern elbowed aside by irritation. She could get very uptight at the risks I seemed to take; risks that always seem so much greater to those watching from the side-lines. "You've just been telling the police all about that, of course?" she enquired innocently, her eyes angry.

"They know about it now," I pointed out. "Things didn't work out quite the way I intended. I promise I expected to be here earlier with a verbatim account. You were going to be the first to know. How I handed this guy – Ellen Longstaff's former husband – over to the police, complete with full confession. However, I did the next best thing. I phoned them and dropped the evidence right in their laps ..."

"You mean the murderer, and the chap he stabbed?"

"Everything they could need – including fingerprints on the knife handle."

"What has all this got to do with Tony Longstaff?"

"I'm not sure yet. All I know is that he's dead."

She winced at the shock. After a couple of minutes she asked what had happened to him.

Reluctant to give her nightmares by outlining my theory, I hedged. "Again, I'm not sure. I think he was drowned in the jacuzzi we took such a dislike to ... "

"But why?"

I did not know where to start. "Ellen's first husband was James Farini, the film producer. Farini went to see Longstaff about finance for his next film. Longstaff turned him down, and an hour or so later he was dead

– yet that doesn't seem a very likely reason. Farini is no nut. I can't see him killing someone in a fit of pique ..."

"How much of this do the police know – if any?

I did not answer, but her challenging stare prompted a sheepish grin.

"You mean you suspected Farini was the killer, and you still went after him alone?" she demanded.

I wriggled uncomfortably at the depth of her indignation. "It was too complicated to explain to anyone. I was already involved. You wouldn't expect me to turn a blind eye ... ?"

"Nelson did."

"Not for the reason you mean ... "

"Well *he* was an idiot too," she said, blithely correcting herself. "Do you care if I end up like Lady Hamilton – in the gutter?"

"Emma Hamilton was just a pretty face. You've got a brain to match and, without me to worry about, you would simply progress to even bigger and better advertising agencies."

She rewarded me for the compliment with a kiss. "You've got a point. But I still don't see why you always have to put *your* head on the chopping-block? That's twice you could have been killed, and what have you got to show for it? Is anyone *ever* likely to be charged with Tony's murder?"

I shook my head. "But that's life. The loose ends don't always tie up neatly. There must be hundreds of unsolved crimes on the police files. I'll be happy if they get Farini for the attempted murder of Stephen Gorton."

"Who is Stephen Gorton?"

I groaned. "This is where we came in! I'll tell you in the morning."

There was nothing in the morning papers about the stabbing, but I suspected that was because there had been insufficient time for the story to be filed. I asked Laura to check later in the London evening paper, and on the drive back to Dorset I kept the car radio tuned to the news broadcasts – but I waited in vain. A stabbing was hardly sensational, of course, but I would have thought it merited a paragraph or two. However, short of ringing someone like George Kester on the *Chronicle* – and it might have been difficult to explain how I knew about a chargeable offence that had not yet been reported – there was nothing I could do about it for the moment.

In fact, my morning paper carried a short piece in the following day's edition and that left me even more frustrated. The paragraph on page five simply read:

> 'London antiquarian bookseller, Stephen Gorton, was in the intensive care unit of Willesden General Hospital today, after being found with stab wounds in his shop off Cricklewood Broadway. Police believe Mr Gorton may have disturbed burglars during the night, and have not ruled out a possible connection with a series of break-ins at art and antique dealers in North West London during the past year.'

The report ended so abruptly that for a moment or two I was tempted to see if there had been an error in typesetting or the page make-up and if the rest of the report was erroneously tagged on to the bottom of another news story. The standard of production had deteriorated in recent years through an apparent shortage of proof-readers and such mistakes were no longer infrequent.

What had to be missing was a final sentence – and I could see it so clearly in my mind – reading:

'A man is helping police with their enquiries.'

newspaper jargon for saying that the assailant had been detained. But the ridiculous link with other break-ins and robberies appeared to rule out any printer's error.

I was stunned. There was only one feasible explanation – that the police had not found Farini. And since I was confident he could not have left the premises under his own steam, the implication was that Ellen had returned in the nick of time to rescue him. I cursed myself for not having tidied up loose ends at the appropriate time; going straight to Ellen's place instead of to Laura, using tiredness as an excuse for complacency.

Even so, I could not just assume Ellen had got Farini out, especially since he had told her to remain out of sight. I had to discover what really happened. There were several options open to me and I evaluated them in order:

I could phone George Kester or the Chronicale crime reporter. The drawback was that they would expect information in return and for the moment I had nothing to give.

I could pay Gorton a visit in hospital – if he was still alive. The snag here was that the local police might have left someone to keep an eye on him, or to take a statement when he had sufficiently recovered.

I could try the old-pals act on Inspector Murdoch – but although he was a friend I did not dare tell him of the way I had interfered with the evidence – especially the bit about ensuring Farini's fingerprints were on the knife.

The alternative was to see if Farini was now at home, or with Ellen. All was not lost. Although he had not been caught red-handed, I doubted if there had been time for him or his accomplice to wipe the fingerprints off the knife – and that could still be an important exhibit in his future prosecution – especially if Gorton could somehow be prevailed upon to identify him as his attacker.

Nothing was to be gained by dashing off in all directions at once and I decided to sit tight for a few days until I had thought of the best move. But again fate took a hand when two of my options – obviously impatient for action – presented themselves to me on a plate.

The first came in the form of a note from Ellen inviting me to join her "and a few friends" at Longlands on Saturday – two days' time. The message was typed on one of those decorative printed invitation cards, but signed in her flamboyant hand with the addition of a couple of words written in capitals: DO COME!

A week or two earlier I might have been flattered by the invitation. Now I had only one thought – that she and Farini were desperate enough to have another go at getting rid of me. It may just have been a remarkable coincidence, but I could not help wondering if "a few friends" was a reference to Farini and his evil-looking pets.

Allowing my imagination to run riot I found myself swimming underwater in the jacuzzi – at least twenty feet deep and finding my limbs encircled by a giant boa constrictor, ten times the size of Farini's snakes. Through the glass sides of the pool I could see him grinning at me, holding his arms wide to indicate how big his pets had grown. I wondered what they were doing in the water and suddenly it vanished to be replaced by a school of piranhas. I was carrying a knife, Tarzan fashion, between my teeth, but realising how ineffective it would be against hundreds of tiny fish I used it instead to cut a hole in the glass – through which the water and fish were instantly sucked out. On dry land again, I came face to face with Nero, more savage than ever – saliva dripping from his jaws as he contemplated the meal I was about to provide. But this time I was ready for him – the stick of chewing-gum I proffered as a gesture of goodwill was really a mint-flavoured glue.

I came to my senses hoping that Farini and Ellen could be overcome with the same sense of omnipotence. But I knew it would not be as simple as that, and for once I intended to cover my rear. Since Ellen had referred to "a few friends", I would be justified in taking Laura, if she was available, as my companion. However, I doubted whether there would be any socialising, in fact, and I did not want to expose Laura to unnecessary danger. I had been invited for early afternoon, so I could arrange to meet Laura there at (say) four o'clock. If it was a genuine social gathering she would obviously stay, but if for any reason I was not there I would arrange for her to phone Inspector Murdoch.

And speak of the devil, who should walk into the shop to interrupt my planning, but Murdoch! I was usually pleased to see him anyway and did not conceal my pleasure, but his answering smile was a little thin. I recognised his 'on duty' manner, and wondered what he wanted. "What's this – a raid?" I demanded.

It was part of our routine banter and normally he would have capped my opening lead; instead he did his best to keep a straight face. "A raid? Heaven knows, what we would find? There was a time when a town's bookseller was a pillar of respectability. It was the *bookmaker* who flirted with the law. Now we don't know who to watch … "

I raised my eyes to the ceiling. "What has upset you now?" Despite his solemnity I could not help pulling his leg. "Someone complained I'm selling pornography? It's a lie."

He favoured me with a half-smile. "You should know I wouldn't be here about books. I always get lumbered with your *other* activities ... nothing as worthy as bookselling."

I groaned. "What am I supposed to have done?" For a worrying second I wondered if his call had anything to do with the stabbing.

"Today I'm representing the Ardley CID messenger service. We've been asked – just for a change – to take a statement for another police force. 'Claims he runs the local bookshop' they told us. I didn't let on it's only something you do in your spare time ... "

The "spare time" crack rankled, in view of the ten-hour days I regularly put in. "What *am* I supposed to do with the rest of my time?"

Having succeeded in getting under my skin, Murdoch allowed himself a broader smile. "We're working on that. My theory is that you are an *agent provocateur* despatched about the countryside by the Home Secretary to keep the police on their toes."

"What's wrong with that?"

"I would be all in favour – if it wasn't for the fact that the resulting investigation always ends up in my lap. Wherever you happen to be ... abusing the law – or, to be fair, provoking some other individual into breaking the law – it is always me who ends up taking statements. It's becoming a full-time occupation."

"Go on," I declared. "You know you like coming here. I don't charge you for reading the comics."

"I've read them all by now ... "

"Oh? Well, unless I can interest you in some quality porn, it will have to be strictly business today."

"I'll settle for a coffee," he said, more like his usual self.

Over coffee and Madeira-cake – he had obviously timed his visit well – Murdoch finally got round to revealing that the statement was in connection with the attack made on me in the conference room of Allman & Spinks. So much had since happened that the incident had receded in my memory. I had to run through the sequence of events in my mind before I could remember the detail. Of course it gave the wrong impression, and Murdoch could not help a cutting aside: "I know you would not lie to me, but just to refresh your memory, we need the *whole* truth, not just selections."

I laughed to cover my confusion while I tried to decide just that – how much I could tell him. There was no need to conceal anything about the attack itself, but I was reluctant to name or even involve Gorton until I knew what had happened after the stabbing. I decided, as usual, to play it by ear and described the collection, the reason for my presence, and the totally unexpected assault.

Murdoch looked up from his notebook wide-eyed. "I've never known anyone as accident-prone. And they always happen out of the blue. You attract violence like a magnet."

I did not comment and when he asked for a likely motive I tried to be helpful. He asked if I had passed on my suspicions to anyone else and did not hide is irritation when I pointed out that there had been no-one to tell. " ... Apart from David Morgan, the chap in charge of the company's security. Naturally, we compared notes."

"Then let's hope he doesn't keep his cards as close to his chest as you."

I explained what had happened to Morgan and he was suddenly revitalised; he was no longer merely going through the motions of taking a routine statement. "Morgan's death is presumably more than a coincidence. Has no-one asked any pertinent questions?"

I shrugged. "The trouble with police investigations – unless it's something massive like a murder enquiry – is that it can be incredibly fragmented. You've got the Hampshire CID making enquiries about Longstaff's disappearance, the Ealing division of the 'Met' looking into a suspected hit-and-run, and ... " I managed to stop myself from referring to a brand-new investigation by Cricklewood police into the stabbing.

"And ... ?" he urged, suspecting there was more, but I shook my head and he closed his notebook. "We had better start fitting the pieces of the jigsaw together," he said, adding with more than a hint of sarcasm. "No doubt you'll pass on a few more helpful tips when you're ready ... ?"

I was in a quandary. The duel with Farini had turned into a vendetta and if he had not already been detained by the police I wanted another crack at him, without their getting in my way. I could normally rely on Murdoch's discretion, but once he was in possession of the facts he could not be expected to do nothing until I had settled a personal score. As soon as he knew the connection between Longstaff and Gorton, and the common link with Farini, it would become a full-scale police enquiry and I would be brushed aside.

On the other hand, Murdoch was able to obtain information that could create all sorts of problems for me – such as trying to find the car that had run down David Morgan. If I gave him a few leads that bore fruit, we might then be in a position to exchange information.

I decided to tell him about the fraud Longstaff had planned and how it had operated. I did not name Gorton. Murdoch, typically, took the disclosure in his stride without comment, although in the course of my explanation he asked a number of pertinent questions. Jumping to Morgan's death I admitted that the security man was the only person with whom I had shared that information. "As you commented, it has to be more than a coincidence that he is now dead. Unfortunately, because of the misleading circumstances … " I broke off to explain the uncorrected assumption that Morgan had been out jogging – "the local police had no reason to believe that the incident was any more than a hit-and-run. They have had no real incentive to trace that car … "

"It's never easy," Murdoch interrupted, "unless it was a stolen car, later abandoned."

"Even then it is a matter of attitude. I had a car stolen once … taken by youngsters for a joy-ride … and that was found with quite a bit of damage, but the police didn't want to know. I have a feeling that our villain is too shrewd to have risked damaging his own car – so the odds are that it *was* stolen … "

"A 'feeling'? speculated Murdoch. "You wouldn't happen to *know* who the driver was?"

"No." I matched his stare, my conscience clear. I had my suspicions, but I did not *know*.

Murdoch grunted. "I won't remind you about the seriousness of withholding evidence … We've been through all that before."

"When I have something the police would regard as

evidence I promise you will be the first to know. Meanwhile, perhaps we can keep in touch.?"

He nodded, and I was reassured, as though I had taken out insurance cover.

Longlands was even more impressive than I had remembered. It was not only the majestic beauty of the house and its grounds, but the sense of timelessness that no human tragedy can affect. Longlands had an identity of its own untouched by the purpose to which it had been put. As a matter of fact, there had been only three families in residence until 1910 when the bachelor Lord Connaught moved to a smaller residence in London and it became a boys' boarding-school. In World War II it was taken over by the War Office and then followed years of limbo during which the place was allowed to run down before Longstaff bought it for a knock-down price, something less than the annual cost of maintenance. If Ellen had any sense she would do a deal with the National Trust; get them to take it off her hands. In my view, monuments like Longlands belonged to the nation.

As a rule I try not to arrive at parties too early, but the invitation had been rather vague, and judging by the forecourt I seemed to be the first guest. Ellen's red mini parked by the front entrance was the only car in evidence, tending to confirm my initial suspicion that she had not invited anyone else. I wondered what her tack would be. Seduction, perhaps? To win me over to her side ... with Farini ... or even against him? The prospect was intriguing, but I used the memory of David Morgan to damp down the excitement.

Nevertheless, Ellen Longstaff was a desirable woman, and when the door was opened – and it was not she who stood there – I could not help feeling a tinge of disappointment. It was her daughter, Jacintha, who invited me in. The girl appeared to have forgotten her rudeness at our last meeting and greeted me as a long lost friend. I have to admit that forgiveness comes a little easier when the guilty party looks anything like Jacintha.

"You are Hugo Diringer's friend, aren't you?" she enquired sweetly, justifying her interest, but merely reminding me of how her mind worked. "Ellen has been held up. She asked me to get here early to act as hostess. I'm not as good as her, of course, but at least while we are alone I promise to give you my entire attention ... "

There was a hint of intimacy about the promise that made my sap rise. I recalled my first sight of her in the sweat-stained shirt, and how even her step-father had reacted. "Step-father ... " the relationship reminded me that her real father was Farini, and I wondered what *that* relationship was. Ellen pretended to despise him, but I no longer believed her. Suddenly I recalled the occasion I had seen her kiss the middle-aged man who had called on her when her mother was out. The assumption that he had been her lover was wrong; he had been her father. I realised now why on my meeting Farini his face and bearing had seemed familiar.

So they *were* on friendly terms! But enough to help him in a criminal act? Surreptitiously I studied her again. She did not strike me as being devious – too transparently shallow. The more intelligent Ellen still seemed to be the better bet, but meanwhile it would be safer to treat both with equal respect. And when Jacintha led me straight to the bar in the drawing-room I waited to see what she was drinking before asking for the same. It happened to be a slimline tonic

– not something I would normally drink for choice – but she did not comment, so I had to put up with it.

"Where is everyone?" I asked. "Your mother mentioned a few friends ... "

"Only half a dozen, including us," she confessed. "John Halford and his girlfriend ... an absolutely stunning model who calls herself Annabel. She's impossibly beautiful, but not very bright ... not that you will notice; men never do. They are bringing Ellen in their car. Then there are the Mertons – husband and wife in their early forties – who live on the other side of the village. They are invariably the nearest, and consequently always the last to arrive. So it seems that Fate has thrust us together for the next hour or so ... "

"Alone?" I speculated.

"Do you mind?" The question was posed with a pout that was so provocative that I found it difficult not to laugh. The expression was like an over-the-top imitation of Marilyn Monroe and it was not until I caught her eye that she smiled and I realised that I had misjudged her. She had a sense of humour and that had to raise her a few notches in my estimation.

I relaxed slightly, but not enough to take any chances, and it was only when I noticed an unopened bottle of Scotch that I decided to risk changing to whisky. The instinctive caution reminded me why I had come, and I wondered how Farini might be linked with my presence at Longlands. I asked if she saw her father often.

"When did I last see my father?" she mimicked, and again I was surprised to know that she had even heard of the famous painting.

"Something like that."

She appeared to give it some thought. "'Bout three weeks ago. Came round to the house when Ellen was at the theatre. She is a bit bitter about the break-up, so I don't usually tell her about out meetings."

"Did the break-up affect you very much at the time?"

"Of course. I was at an impressionable age. I knew I had to come to terms with it, but it was tough for a while – I missed Jimmy a lot ..."

"What sort of man is he? Talented, obviously ... I know about his film-making. I meant as a father?"

I waited for her to impose a distance between them, to maintain that as adults they had nothing in common, but she was generous in her praise. "A shrink would tell me I've got a father-fixation – that I'll end up marrying an old man – a surrogate father." She smiled. "Relax, Matt, you're safe – you are too young!"

I returned the smile, but made no comment, anxious to stay with Farini. "It must have been a blow when your mother remarried?"

"Not as much as people expected. I was sixteen ... physically a woman. I could see myself replacing Ellen in my father's affections, so that couldn't be bad. On the other hand, she always doted on me. One of the reasons she married Tony was to guarantee my future security ..."

"What did you think of him?"

"Tony?" She laughed. "He was nice enough. Very generous, of course, to people he liked. Bit of a groper at times, but I can't say it ever bothered me."

Our eyes met and she stared at me. I found it difficult not to look away. It was not the sexual challenge that scared me; more that my feelings towards her were ambiguous. I had disliked her originally; now I was not so sure. I was also puzzled by her reference to Longstaff in the past tense;

although, equally, it could merely have been because that had been the way I phrased my question.

She seemed to be aware of my indecision and sighed plaintively. "I thought all this cross-examination was leading to something ... a proposal of some sort ... ?"

"You just said I was too young."

" ... To make an honest woman of me! *I* wasn't thinking of anything as long-term or straitlaced as that."

"What did you have in mind?"

"As acting hostess I have to entertain *you*. If you're not going to make advances, what about some other activity? Fancy a swim?"

"Not really, thanks. I will – to keep you company – but a couple of minutes under the shower is about all the cold water I can take for pleasure."

"It is a bit cold today, we haven't turned the heating on. What about the jacuzzi? That'll be warm ... "

I thought of Longstaff and the indescribable horror that had probably befallen him and it was all I could do not to show my revulsion. "No thanks. What else is on the menu?"

"Squash?"

The idea was much more appealing. My game is tennis, but I enjoy an occasional game of squash or badminton, provided my opponent is not too skilled. I am too competitive to enjoy being thrashed too conclusively. "What about gear?" I asked.

"Tony always keeps spare equipment and clothes in the locker-room. There is bound to be something that fits you."

"Then you're on!" I declared, "provided we're not playing for big stakes."

"I only play for love," she said, taking my hand and squeezing it. Jacintha pouted again for effect and I did not know whether she was laughing with me – or at me. However, I was beginning to warm towards her and when she pointed me in the direction of the locker-room, saying that she was going to turn on the sauna for later, I was quite keen to see which of us would win.

Fired by the competitive spirit, we changed together unselfconsciously and hurried on to the court. I should have realised from her interest in horseriding that Jacintha was a keen sportswoman, and she played squash with considerable verve and skill. In the event, it was pride that prompted me to play above myself and to win 9-7, 9-6, 9-6 in just over an hour. She was the better player technically, but we were equally matched for stamina and my greater power offset her better stroke-play. I was also probably the keener competitor, running as though my life depended on it to retrieve shots that in other circumstances I might have conceded. For someone who does not normally show off I must admit I was not particularly gracious in victory. I even claimed that I had been off-form. But Jacintha accepted defeat in good part and I was immediately ashamed, knowing that I could never look back on my behaviour without embarrassment.

Nevertheless I was very conscious of male dominance as we entered the sauna, enough at least to cover my initial embarrassment. Belonging to a generation still not completely rid of its inhibitions, I wrapped a bath-towel round my waist. I was disappointed but somewhat relieved to see that she had also draped herself in a large towel.

I recalled how Longstaff had complained about the cost of all his 'fixtures and fittings' but inside the sauna was no different to most others. The room was about 10 feet long by 10 feet wide, and the only fitted furniture was a well-finished slatted pine bench running the length of one wall with wooden steps leading to another level at head height above it for those who prefer higher temperatures. There were also three folding canvas chairs as an alternative to the unyielding surface of the pine, a small table on which were piled a few magazines, and spare white towels.

Initially Jacintha seemed as shy as me, and occupied herself adjusting the thermostat and testing the temperature at the two levels before coming back to join me on the lower of the pine benches.

I was conscious of the line across her chest where the white towel cut into her flesh. She followed my gaze and smiled and I guessed she was about to take the initiative. But as I waited expectantly she seemed to stiffen with concentration, as though she was listening for something. She was.

"Can you hear the phone?" she asked.

I could not, but conceded that her ears were probably better than mine.

"Blast!" The downward curve of her full mouth was an indication of her irritation. "It *is* the phone. It's probably Ellen ... I'll have to go."

She took another towel from the pile and sensibly draped it over her head in anticipation of the change in temperature outside. "I'll only be a second," she announced, and to cheer me up went through her pouting routine. "Don't go away," she said with mock coyness.

I lay back on the pine bench and relaxed. The sweat was already pouring off me and I felt pleasantly tired. I wondered what it would be like to doze off and be awakened by Jacintha's naked embrace. But she was back within a couple of minutes, frowning with annoyance.

"Don't tell me ... they're not coming!" I speculated.

She smiled. "No such luck. I wouldn't want you to think I was a prick-teaser, but I'm afraid you'll have to do without me for a bit longer ... "

My disappointment was genuine enough, but I tried not to show it. "What's the problem?"

"That was the Mertons. Their car is being serviced. The garage promised it back today and you can guess the rest. They wanted to know if someone could pick them up. And since there *is* only me, I had to volunteer. Fortunately, it's just down the road; five minutes in the car ... "

"I'll come with you ... "

"No point in both of us catching colds. Stay where you are; they'll probably want to join us anyway ... although it won't be quite the same, obviously."

"All right. How long will you be?"

"Fifteen minutes at the most. If it gets too hot turn the thermostat down – it's on 80°F at the moment – or just come out. There's a shower in the cubicle next door."

She departed, leaving me with thoughts of what might have been. I had to concede that Jacintha had grown on me. There was probably no greater depth to her than I had first imagined, but when she bothered, she was undeniably good company.

The heat was beginning to be a little oppressive and I sprinkled some cold water from the small watering-can on to the heated lava rock container to create some steam, easing the tightness on my chest. It started me thinking about saunas, comparing them with the once fashionable Turkish steam baths. I remembered sitting in steam-filled rooms, the sweat pouring off me in torrents, amazed that I should be enjoying the experience, and wondered which of the systems was the most effective. I was certainly sweating heavily now. I reckoned I could afford to lose at least seven pounds of flab, but trouble was that any fluid I lost now would be replaced by the first glass of water I drank later. I decided to persevere; to put up with the discomfort.

Time is a strange phenomenon. When we have to wait for something, time drags interminably; when we are doing absolutely nothing, drifting on the astral plane or whatever it is, time seems to be suspended; of no importance whatsoever. I continued to lie on my back, in a state of suspended animation, until I was conscious that it had become unpleasantly hot. I could almost 'feel' the heat against my skin.

I got up and checked the thermostat. It was registering just over 80°F, which should not have been too uncomfortable, but I realised I might be overdoing it for the first time in ages, so I turned it down and put some more water on the grey rocks. I was getting a little bored and there seemed little point in waiting for the others to arrive – to start all over again. Apart from the boredom, I would end up like a lobster.

Moderation Coll, I rebuked myself, deciding to call it a day. There seemed no point in wasting electricity, so I turned the thermostat right down and took a quick look round to ensure that everything was in order before leaving. At least, that was my intention, but the door was stuck. I turned the handle and put my weight against the wood, but it would not budge.

I gave a mental shrug of the shoulders and prepared to suffer a little, waiting for the others to return and open the door. But despite the fact that the thermostat was now down to the minimum level the temperature gauge was registering 110°F. In fact, it seemed to be getting hotter by the minute. As I looked at the red temperature needle, the penny suddenly dropped and I realised that the door was not stuck – but locked. It seemed that Jacintha had no intention of coming back until I was well and truly baked. The analogy caused me to panic slightly. If the thermostat was not working – or had been deliberately broken – and the temperature continued to rise, I would die. Despite myself I could not help wondering what would happen, whether my blood would start to boil or perhaps my lungs ...? With any luck I would lose consciousness first. Perhaps it was just as well I was not too good at biology. She ... or presumably her father ... had to be congratulated on the cleverness of their plan because my death would appear to have been from natural causes. She could either claim that she had left me for ten minutes and returned to find me dead, or even that we had been in the sauna together and that she thought I had fallen asleep. The collapse might even be attributed to the strenuous games of squash we had played first.

I looked round for a means of escape, but the room was sealed and the glass panel in the door was made of a reinforced material that might withstand the force of a sledgehammer. I did not have a sledgehammer, but there was some pretty solid-looking pine. I was not too optimistic, but it was better than nothing. I knew a little karate and I suppose there are one or two masters of the art around who could have smashed through the bench with a blow from their fist, but I was certainly not one of them. I examined the structure carefully and realised that the only way to break it without proper tools was to apply pressure – preferably with force – to the corner joints where the legs met the beam going across. I bandaged my feet with towels, protecting them as much as possible, and launched an assault on the joints. After little more than a dozen or so blows with my heel I was forced to concede defeat; the whole of the heel and sole areas of both feet were painfully bruised and the pain was beginning to spread through my ankles to both shins.

Intent on my task, I was conscious only of the pain in my legs, but as soon as I stopped I found myself breathing heavily from my exertions and finding that the intake of hot air was another source of discomfort. I poured more water over the lava rocks, but even the steam no longer gave any relief.

The only usable implement left was the ladder linking the two seating levels. It was fixed securely by means of metal clasps gripping the rungs. Having tried to pull it away and, not having the strength, I climbed on to the bottom seat, crouching between the two levels, and then braced my back against the ladder. I took a deep breath, painful though it was, counted to three and pushed with my back and legs. The explosive weight of my body made all the difference and the clasps gave way.

The ladder was four feet long with the protruding side pieces about two square inches of solid wood. Placing it lengthwise over my shoulder, I used it as a battering-ram. It took nearly a dozen charges, not all of them on target, before the glass cracked. Then with fresh heart, I worked on the cracking pane until there were a couple of small holes. Thin pieces of wire built into the glass layers prevented it from disintegrating completely, but the rush of cool air was reward enough. Pressing my face as close to the broken window as I dared, I peered out and saw the key protruding from the lock outside the door. It was impossible for me to reach it, but the supply of fresh air meant that the immediate crisis was over. I wrapped myself in towels from top to toe and stood as close to the draught of cold air as possible.

I was still there fifteen minutes later when I heard the smash of glass in another part of the house. My enemies did not need to smash anything to gain entry, so I called for help. Seconds later the cavalry arrived in the form of Laura Cottingham. I always said that she had a remarkable sense of timing.

Eleven

Unable to get a reply to her persistent knocking, Laura had broken into the house. Because I was fearful of exposing her to danger I had insisted that she did nothing rash – simply drive to the nearest telephone box to call Inspector Murdoch, who would have got the local police on the spot without delay. Now I was thankful that she had disobeyed me and used her initiative.

As I pointed out to her, the facts might seem self-evident but it would be almost impossible to substantiate allegations that the locked door and faulty thermostat had been deliberately engineered. Besides, I was too embarrassed to have been caught with my pants down (and more!) yet again. Typically Laura did not ask what I was doing in the sauna with Jacintha and, although I had no reason to be ashamed of my behaviour, I was more than a little conscious of my gullibility.

Having cooled down, I took a lukewarm shower and

then dressed. I took my time, hoping that Jacintha would return. I intended to play it cool (if I could ever be cool again), maintaining that I had left the sauna before noticing anything unusual. It would be interesting to see how she coped with the shock. But soon it became apparent that she would not make the same mistake as I had a few days earlier – taking it for granted that Farini would be found by the police at Gorton's shop. I decided to cut my losses and leave.

Looking for a release for my pent-up frustrations, I toyed with the idea of fetching pillows from a bedroom and draping them in towels, so that in the sauna they would pass for a crumpled body. It seemed an amusing idea until I realised that Jacintha would guess what had happened the moment she returned and saw that my car had gone.

Laura and I used our own cars to get back to Ardley and in the midst of my anger at Farini and his daughter I wondered what would have happened if Laura had not turned up right on cue. I relied on her in more ways than one and seldom showed my appreciation. I decided to make it up to her as soon as possible, perhaps by using what remained of Longstaff's commission to treat us both to a decent holiday abroad. After my experiences of the past few weeks I felt I could do with a complete break – not to say convalescence.

With a conscience marginally appeased, my thoughts returned to Farini. I had been overconfident from the start, assuming that I could outsmart him simply by waiting for his move and then reacting like an avenging angel. I have always had good reflexes, which makes me a natural counter-puncher – but since that tack had let me down, from now on I would have to make the play. If there were any traps to be set, they would be sprung by me.

Back at Ardley, I put Laura in the picture. To appease her, I agreed to include Murdoch in my plans – although to be truthful, it was not merely to satisfy her concern. I was more than ready to put my personal pride on one side – to be more detached in my attitude. Rather typically, I went to the other extreme – recruiting outside help in addition to Murdoch, who, on reflection, did not have to be involved until the last moment.

First, I needed to secure the co-operation of Allman & Spinks, and this I obtained through a single phone call to Chris Jenkins of the PR department. The rest of my 'team' would be made up by two regular customers who had become friends. One was John Weatherall, managing director of a local sports shop who owned one of the country's largest collections of books on fish and fishing. John's interest was primarily in cold-water fish, but he would know *where* to find out what I needed to know about tropical waters. The other was Rodney Bennett, an actor I had met through Laura and whose collection on the Napoleonic Wars had been handsomely supplemented by a number of rare volumes I had found for him. My call on this occasion was nothing to do with books; I needed his professional services.

When my plan was practically complete I made separate calls to Farini, Ellen and Jacintha. Since I was now calling the tune, the meeting had to be on my home territory, so I extended invitations they would find difficult to refuse.

The showdown took place the following Saturday so that Charlie Appleton could look after the shop, leaving me free to 'entertain' my visitors from London. Sunday might have been even better, but I needed

Murdoch in attendance and could hardly expect him to give up a free day for what might still be a false alarm if my plan backfired.

It was just as well that I waited for them in the shop because Farini turned up with Nero in attendance, and I did not want to keep looking over my shoulder, or risk him prowling about until he found Murdoch's hiding-place. I intercepted them at the front door and persuaded Farini that Nero should be given the run of the garden. Again he surprised me. I had assumed the dog was there for his protection, but it seemed he merely wanted to give the dog a change of scenery and claimed to welcome the opportunity for him to run free.

We spent ten minutes in the shop; him browsing and me spouting banal pleasantries about the weather and the car journey from London. It was as though we were rehearsing the pre-fight preliminaries, when the referee issues the last-minute instructions that no-one hears – or even listens to. The first tentative sparring began when I told him I was expecting Jacintha and Ellen and he feigned a mild surprise that did not fool me for a second. We were still only going through the motions, keeping our trump cards well concealed.

I took him into my living-room immediately behind the shop, drawing his attention to some rather special books lodged in relative safety, well away from the insidious fingers of the shoplifters who plague bookshops. Inevitably, his eyes fell on a small section of fishing books – some of which I had borrowed from a dealer friend specialising in South American topography and natural history – and quickly focussed on a couple of items that had been 'planted' for his benefit.

They were rare 19th-century works on the Amazon

river, bound in contemporary morocco and with the gilt lettering on the spines still relatively fresh. The first, published in London in 1868, was the two-volume *Highlands of Brazil*, one of the lesser-known works of Sir Richard Burton, remembered today primarily for explorations in Africa and the Middle East, as well as translations of *The Arabian Nights* and other more erotic works. The other was probably the more interesting to Farini, bearing in mind the author's more specialist knowledge – Francis de Gastelnau's *Animaux nouveaux ou rares ... Amerique du Sud*, Paris 1855. There was also another highly specialist item, *Geology and Physical Geography of Brazil*, by C F Hartt, bound as an extract from a larger study of the country.

One of the fascinations of bookselling is that what one bibliophile will discard as worthless, another will pay a small fortune to possess – which is why collectors on their travels can usually pick up what they regard as bargains; items which may have been neglected for months. The art, obviously, from the bookseller's point of view is to save books of 'vertical' interest for collectors on that subject. I knew Farini would give his eye-teeth for the three titles he had taken from their place.

"There is no price in these ... " he said cagily, ready to negotiate, and it was difficult for me to keep a straight face.

"If I were selling them, I would expect around £350 ..."

He was tempted, but presumably not in a position to write a cheque for that amount. "What about individually? The French book ... ?"

I shook my head. "Only as a single lot."

As a serious collector he was wrestling with his

conscience and after a few moments I cut into his train of thought. "Of course, in these rather special circumstances, I might be able to work something out?"

"Such as ... ?"

I smiled. "This afternoon, we shall be discussing a certain business matter. If I get what I regard as a reasonable offer on *that* score, I could be persuaded to throw in the books – as a sort of goodwill *bonus*."

His expression did not change. His singleminded desire for the books obliged him to take the proposal seriously, although he was too shrewd to commit himself at this stage. "If some sort of arrangement could be arrived at over this ... other business matter," he speculated after a few moments. "What sort of figure did you have in mind?"

"The sum is negotiable. Since you are not as affluent as your ex-wife for example – I would be reasonable. I was thinking of £25,000."

"You're crazy!" he exploded. "Even if I was interested where would I find that sort of money?"

" ... And that includes the tape," I added, ignoring the outburst. "I'll play it this afternoon, even if it means distressing the ladies. I don't think there will be any argument after that ... " I spoke confidently, but all the time I was sweating with embarrassment at what Murdoch was thinking. I had warned him to take much of what I said with a pinch of salt but, assuming he was recording the proceedings, it was difficult to see how he would explain the threatened blackmail to his superiors.

Farini was about to respond when we were interrupted by Charlie Appleton with the announcement that 'two ladies' had called to see me. As he ushered them in with his old-world charm I was intrigued by their manner: Ellen subdued, almost sullen, while Jacintha exuded confidence. She kissed her father as though she had expected to see him, and advanced on me quite brazenly. Apparently she had second thoughts when I stepped back with distaste.

When I had telephoned her, Jacintha had been as cool as a cucumber. "What on earth happened to you?" she had demanded, as though I had walked out on her. "After the tremendous build-up I gave you, the Mertons must have thought I was mad." I had not answered, merely explaining why I considered it was in her interests to come to Ardley for a family 'reunion'. Hardly bothering to listen to my reasoning, she announced that she would be *delighted* to see me again.

For someone as sophisticated as Ellen, she was surprisingly off-balance. She acknowledged Farini as though he was a stranger, not even deigning to shake hands, but the real anger and contempt was reserved for me. It was she who had offered the most resistance on the phone, although I had the impression it was the element of coercion that had upset her. Had the invitation been phrased more gracefully she might have accepted without any fuss.

I asked them to be seated and, conscious of my hypocrisy, thanked them for coming. "Let's be blunt," I began. "This is business; not a social gathering. But that is no reason why we should stand on ceremony. I am in a position to help you; the fact that I expect to be paid must not be allowed to disguise the fact."

"Come to the point!" Ellen exclaimed. "I said on the phone that I didn't know what you were talking about, and I still don't ... "

"You're here, nevertheless," I pointed out.

"To protect the interests of my daughter."

I smiled at a mental picture of sweet and defenceless Jacintha, but said nothing.

Conveniently forgetting that ten minutes earlier he had not been contesting the principle of blackmail – merely the terms – Farini cut in blandly: "Let's hear what the guy has to say, and get it over with."

"That's good advice," I concluded. "The facts are these. Anthony Longstaff is dead. He's been dead from the start."

"I don't know where you get your information," Ellen retorted, "the police haven't said a word to me?"

"He was murdered by your former husband. What I don't know yet is which of you ladies helped him."

Farini laughed.

I ignored him. "David Morgan was also murdered by the same team… "

I was interrupted by a hoot of derision from Ellen. "We know about David. There's no mystery about it … the police say it was an accident … "

"The inquest was adjourned," I pointed out. "You'll find that coroners don't record verdicts of 'accidental death' when it was deliberate. David was killed because he knew too much … "

Her face having drained of colour, she fell silent.

"As I said, the three of you would not have come all this way if you had nothing to hide – no matter how 'protective' you feel towards each other."

"If someone accused *you* of murder, wouldn't you be just a little curious?" said Farini.

Ellen was still bewildered. "I thought we were friends … at least, I trusted you. If you suspected me, why didn't you say something?"

"I didn't know the terms of Longstaff's will until a few days ago … in other words, I didn't know the extent to which you and your daughter benefited … "

"The money was coming to us anyway," Jacintha cut in. "Anthony set up a trust fund for me which matures on my thirtieth birthday. I could have waited. I didn't need to kill him."

"You're conveniently forgetting the clause that entitled you to be paid out on his death."

"To hell with policy clauses," Ellen responded. "If I killed Tony I would have found a way that didn't oblige me to wait for at least seven years for him to be declared legally dead."

"That isn't strictly so," I pointed out. "I checked with the insurance company. It seems they are bound by what the courts decide. There is no need to wait – after a reasonable period you can apply to a court for judgement. A couple of years is reasonable."

"If you honestly believe I killed my husband," Ellen said, "I would rather you went to the police."

"But that's what this meeting is all about. It's a toss-up whether my evidence would hold up in a court of law, but it is probably enough to stir the Director of Public Prosecutions to action, and more than enough for the insurance companies. Even if there was no prosecution they would certainly stop payment on both policies and invite you to sue them for the money."

"Get to the point," Farini urged.

"The point is that each of you has benefited from the murders. Because of you, I've lost out and I want to be compensated. I'm not greedy. I want £50,000 from the ladies – after all, you're inheriting small fortunes – and a mere £25,000 from Mr Farini in view of his current financial embarrassment. What do you say, Ellen?"

She shook her head in confusion. "That's blackmail! I can't believe it ..."

I played it tough. "Believe it or not, I'm waiting for an answer ..."

"I'll see you in hell first!"

"Jacintha?"

"I'm inclined to endorse Ellen's sentiments." The reaction was more controlled. Her mother had been outraged, but Jacintha was prepared to listen and call my bluff.

"Farini? Perhaps you ought to talk some sense into them."

He shrugged helplessly. "What can I say? Even if I wanted to pay you off, I don't have that sort of money."

"Are you mad?" interceded Ellen. "What have we got to hide? And even if *you* have, blackmailers are never satisfied. He'll bleed you dry!"

Her opinion of me no longer mattered. I kept silent, waiting for them to squabble among themselves.

"Surprising though it may seem," Farini replied, "I was thinking of *you*. My conscience is as clear as anyone's, but Coll is no more dishonest than the insurance companies. It can't be in our interests to give those bastards an excuse to withhold payment ..."

What could *he* say that would make them do that?" she demanded.

"Exactly," agreed Jacintha. "He's bluffing."

I shrugged. "We shall see. Let's start with David Morgan. At least there is a body." I looked at Ellen. "You never said anything about having an affair with him."

She returned my stare. "Of course not. What business was it of yours?"

"None at all – until he ended up in the mortuary.

But you didn't seem to be terribly upset by his death ..."

"How could you know what I felt?" she retorted. "Was I supposed to turn up at his funeral in widow's weeds? As a matter of fact, it was only out of respect for his mother that I didn't go. Ironically it was Tony who pushed us together. The idea was that if I was too distracted by a young admirer I wouldn't have time to notice his philandering."

"As you said, that's none of my business. What is more to the point, Morgan had no secrets from you. He was killed because he found a tape-recording of your husband discussing finance for your *ex*-husband's next film. If he told you that ... "

I did not need to finish: she was obviously startled by the news. Evidently it was one piece of information that Morgan had not passed on. "When was that?" she eventually asked.

I told her. "If nothing else, it demonstrated that Mr Farini was the last person to see your husband alive ..."

"So what?" Farini cut in. "He was fine when I left him on the road to London."

" ... and with other information now in my possession, it proves that he was murdered. I'll come to that later. Morgan and I discussed it and he went to see you."

"I told you, he never showed."

I turned to Ellen. "David asked me to go with him. If I had, he would have been alive today."

Farini threw up his hands in apparent exasperation. "Are you saying he scared me so much that I had to kill him? I followed him in my car and ran him down?"

"Something like that."

"Well the forensic people can examine my car any time they like."

"You're not that stupid to use your own car?"

"I'm a film-maker, not a car-thief. Do *you* know how to steal a car? I'm sure I don't."

There was no doubt in my mind that he was involved in some way, but how to prove it? I felt myself floundering. "Doesn't it seem a coincidence that on the day Morgan confronted you he should have been killed in a road accident? Traffic accidents are common enough, admittedly, but not where the car disappears ..."

I glanced at Ellen, who seemed stunned by the cat-and-mouse game. Although she was contemptuous of me she must have realised that there is no smoke without fire, and that I would not be so persistent unless I was sure of my ground. "I bet he even has an alibi – just in case ..." I said for her benefit.

He shrugged. "As a matter of fact I have."

"Then it was your daughter who drove the car. I haven't forgotten the night you drugged me. You phoned someone to bring your car round to Gorton's bookshop. Presumably it was her who went back to get you out before the police arrived ..."

"What on earth are you talking about?" demanded Ellen.

"At the time I thought it was you," I admitted, "but since then it's begun to fall into place."

"What has ... ?" she insisted.

"I get the impression you don't often see your ex-husband, so let's talk about Jacintha for a minute. Did you ever mention Stephen Gorton to her?"

"Stephen Gorton ... ?"

I reminded her of the circumstances in which she had

met the bookseller.

She pondered on the question for a moment before trying to duck it. "I ... I can't remember."

She was lying, but I did not push it any further. "They set out to frame me for Gorton's murder."

"*Us* frame *him*!" cried Farini. "How many more murders are you trying to pin on us?"

Since I was in danger of losing credibility I gave Ellen only the briefest account of what had happened. It still sounded far-fetched even to my ears, but my case was strengthened because she knew of Gorton's involvement in the initial fraud. "Gorton is the only other person who knows the truth, but he'll keep quiet so long as he can escape being charged with the assault on me at the offices of Allman & Spinks ... "

"*That* was the man who put you in hospital?"

I had been concentrating so much on them that I had not given the hiding Murdoch much thought; now I had visions of him fuming at the latest disclosure. Not for the first time he had caught me out 'forgetting' vital evidence, but I would have to deal with that problem later.

"The point is that Farini needed help – and Jacintha was the person he called upon then. Can you remember if she ever asked you where David Morgan lived?"

She did not reply, but the sudden realisation registered as pain on her face.

I leaned on her a little harder. "David's mother said he received a telephone call late at night, just as she was ready for bed. He told her he was going out for a minute, and we can be pretty certain that he was going to a public telephone, fifty yards up the road. From the way he left the house in such a hurry, we can also assume he thought the message was from you. It's not important. What matters is that your daughter was waiting – and ran him down."

"I can't believe that ... " Ellen retorted, but her eyes went to Jacintha, praying for a convincing denial.

The girl laughed at her concern. "He'll be telling us next that the police found my fingerprints on the steering-wheel."

"I've no need to lie to you, because I've got the facts. They've found the car. It belongs to a young idiot called Freddie Althorpe." I turned to Ellen. "The family live a few streets away from you; do you know the boy?"

She shook her head, and I continued: "The local police do. He's what you might call an upper-class hooligan. Caught him only recently driving while disqualified, so this time they were ready to throw the book at him – even though he claimed his car had been stolen. Fortunately for Althorpe he had an alibi. Of course the police did not know then that someone had a *motive* for killing David, so I asked if Althorpe was a loner, or whether he moved with other young shits. What do you think I discovered?"

Jacintha had gone pale and I sensed I had hit the mark. In that instant Farini's eyes met mine. He knew his daughter was in trouble. Forcing a hollow laugh he insisted I was clutching at straws, but the hint of desperation in his face gave me fresh hope.

The information about Althorpe had been supplied by Murdoch, but now I embellished the facts a little. "I rang Althorpe – said I was a friend of a friend – and asked for Jacintha's telephone number. The cunning devil wouldn't give it to me, but there was no question he knew her. I don't know *how* you got the car ... whether you actually asked if you could borrow it, or whether you took it without his knowledge, but ... "

Jacintha was breathing heavily, near to panic. "It's not true."

"The little toe-rag hadn't been driving for months, but the police said the car had been used fairly regularly. My bet is that several of his friends have spare keys – including you." The girl's self-confidence had already evaporated, but I felt no sympathy.

Ellen looked even more distraught. She knew now – if she had not already suspected – that the child she had spoiled was beyond redemption. Farini was also distressed at the way that Jacintha's brittle composure had snapped, but quickly recovered. He smiled benignly at the women. "*Now* you can see what I meant about paying this guy off. Even a madman can sound convincing. He'll soon have *me* believing that rubbish. Why don't we pay him off, and sleep easier at nights?"

Ellen, concerned for her daughter, responded positively. She looked at me earnestly and apologised for her earlier belligerence. "How do we know you would keep quiet?"

I was embarrassed at the way I had misjudged her. "You would pay blackmail to protect your daughter?"

She nodded. "For a guarantee that he wouldn't try it again."

I shook my head. "It was an act. I only used it to get you all here."

"You don't want money?"

"Nor would I cover up murder ... "

Jacintha was slumped in her chair, dazed and uncaring. Ellen moved over to shake her by the shoulders. "*Say* something. Say it wasn't you." But the girl didn't respond.

I glanced at Farini with contempt. "I notice you're keeping quiet. She did it for you, but you're only concerned with saving your own skin."

Before Farini could respond we were interrupted by Charlie announcing the arrival of John Weatherall. I welcomed him effusively, launching a fresh charade for the benefit; all the time closely watching their reactions. Farini was patently relieved at the temporary respite, but Ellen was in no mood to meet strangers and Jacintha did not even look up.

I introduced everyone: Weatherall as an authority on tropical fish, which he was not; Farini more honestly.

"You've come at a fortuitous moment, John," I told him. "Mr Farini is making a wonderfully exciting film in which a murderer wants to get rid of the body – something a bit more original than burying it in the garden. One of the suggestions is to drown the victim, and fill the pool with piranhas. Could our murderer get away with that?"

"*Swimming*-pool?" Weatherall speculated. I knew from his expression that he had done his homework, but he reacted as though the question presented a challenge, thinking about it for two or three minutes before nodding. "In theory."

Farini's expression showed interest, but he remained silent and it was impossible to know what was going on in his mind. Almost certainly, his knowledge of the subject was greater than Weatherall's, and it was that awareness that decided my approach – to provoke him by insulting his expertise. "In *practice*, what are the problems?" I asked Weatherall.

"Piranhas are tropical fish. The average swimming-pool is far too cold for them ... "

"Then for the sake of Mr Farini's plot, let's make it a jacuzzi ... "

He nodded enthusiastically. "*Much* better. They can be quite docile in tranquil water, but the jets and bubbles would certainly animate them. Mind you, they would have to be *starving* to get through a meal of that size, and hungry piranhas don't stand on ceremony – they would eat each other first ..."

"We would make our killer an expert. Could he not keep them sedated until the right moment?"

"There are several methods ... "

Farini's irritation bubbled over. "You're still theorising," he interceded. "I saw piranhas at first hand in Brazil, and all those wild stories about them devouring horses and cows that strayed into the river are not so easy to substantiate. You would need *hundreds*.

"You would need 25-30 to cope with something smaller, like a man."

"I disagree," insisted Farini, "at least not in one session. And since that would fill them up for *days*, what would you do with the rest of the body?"

I noticed that Jacintha was looking decidedly ill and pointed her in the direction of the ground-floor toilet, hoping that Murdoch would stay out of sight. Ellen was too spellbound by the discussion and its implication to notice her leave.

"Perhaps you're right," conceded Weatherall, "but there must be a way ... "

"Exactly," I echoed. "The chances are that an expert like that would be in and out of the zoo – and what better place could there be for dumping what was left of the body ... ?"

At that point, Jacintha returned, her face deathly white and pinched with strain. She had been sick, but looked as though the worst was not yet over. Despite what she had done, I felt a tinge of sympathy. Even if

Farini had taken her into his confidence I doubted whether she realised the extent of his madness; in any case Morgan and Gorton had been strangers, but she had liked her step-father. Her obvious distress also affected Ellen, who, having held herself on a tight rein, was now reminded of her priorities. Whatever she felt about Longstaff's death, her primary concern was to protect her daughter. She half rose to go to her, but the girl gestured that she wanted to be left alone.

I decided there was little more to achieve by pursuing speculation about what might have happened in the jacuzzi. I had succeeded in undermining the foundation of whatever their relationship had been. Ending the façade, I told Weatherall his input had been invaluable and passed him back to Charlie Appleton.

I returned to Jacintha. "Did you know your father killed Anthony Longstaff?"

She looked to Farini for guidance and getting none she shook her head, unable to bring herself to speak – the mental anguish as apparent as the physical.

Conscious of her vulnerability, I pressed home my advantage. "You may have guessed, but I bet he never spelt it out. You didn't know about the piranhas?"

She shuddered, closing her eyes in a vain effort to shut out the mental picture.

Farini leapt out of his chair. "Leave her alone!" he demanded. He reached her in a couple of strides, squatting on his haunches so that his face was only a few inches from hers. "Don't listen to him, 'Cintha," he whispered soothingly. "He's trying to trick us ... confuse us."

I switched my attention to Ellen. "Who do *you* believe?" When she avoided my eyes, I continued: "Then let's see how much he loves his daughter ... " I produced a tape cassette from my jacket pocket and took it to the music centre set into the bookshelves just behind her chair. I held up the tape theatrically. "That business about the piranhas wasn't just a shot in the dark."

I turned to Farini. "It's all on the tape. The longer it plays, the more Jacintha is going to find out about you."

"You're bluffing," replied Farini, but there was a haunted look about him. He had been worried from the start over what the tape might reveal; now in the face of my confidence he feared the worst.

I shrugged. "I must warn the ladies that it's not for the squeamish, but he has it in his power to stop me at any time." I switched on the tape that Morgan had found:

" … Cosier in here … " Ellen drew in her breath sharply at the sound of her husband's voice, while Jacintha shrank back into her chair, her eyes shut tight.

While the tape played, Farini protested: "It doesn't mean a thing. I *admit* there was a business meeting, but we couldn't reach agreement, so I left … "

"You said before you left him on the road to London … Don't answer, save your breath – it's all here …"

I speeded up the tape to the passage where Longstaff had been critical of Farini's budget – letting it play for a minute or so to give them the 'flavour' of the discussion and then speeding up again. I sensed that Farini was increasingly nervous and debating whether or not to concede defeat.

Longstaff's voice continued " … it's a risk I would be irresponsible to take."

"What if I was to get another director?"

"By all means try me again ..."

As the discussion reached its climax, I studied my audience. Jacintha had her fingers in her ears and, with her eyes tightly shut, was doing her best to suspend her senses; Ellen was licking her lips nervously, judgement still suspended; Farini perspiring freely, his gaze constantly switching from his daughter to me. As our eyes met I detected a note of appeal, but I needed something more positive for the listening Murdoch.

I speeded up the tape again, coming in on Farini. The voice was a little faint as though he had moved away from the hidden microphone. "I've heard a lot about these jacuzzis, but never tried one ..."

"By all means," Longstaff replied, apparently from his original position. "Most uplifting."

"You're looking a bit under the weather. Why don't you join me?"

"Of course. I'd like to ... I'm tired ..."

I pressed the stop button and glanced up at them. "I think we ought to get Jacintha out of here before ..."

"That wasn't me!" cried Farini hoarsely.

I laughed. "Come *on* – don't insult our intelligence!" Announcing that I was warning them for the last time, I speeded up the tape. This time the sound came up on the noise of what might have been a waterfall, although we realised it must be the jacuzzi. In the background we heard a faint cry of pain. It made even my blood run cold, and it triggered off a piercing scream of terror from Jacintha. As I switched off the cassette, Ellen rushed to comfort her, and Charlie stuck his head through the door silently mouthing the question that must have been on the lips of everyone else in the shop. I nodded to reassure him and confronted Farini. "It goes on. How much more do you want her to hear?"

He was exhausted, drained of emotion. When he looked up a shadow of the self-confident film producer, he apologised. "I didn't mean it to happen like that. I've had nightmares ever since."

"Why was it necessary to kill him?"

"Despite the big act, I'm broke. The film was my last chance to get off the floor. 'Cintha wanted to help but she couldn't touch her legacy – and that planted the seed. As well as that I also knew how much Ellen would inherit, and that 'Cintha could always borrow more from here."

"And what about Morgan?"

He shrugged. "It's the *first* that's difficult. After going through all that I had an investment to protect."

He put his arms round his daughter and squeezed her reassuringly. "All I needed was this one film to get me back up there," he said.

The admission was such a relief that I was caught off-balance as he moved away from her and dashed for the music centre. Before I could get to him he removed the tape and stamped on it repeatedly with his heel until it was in shreds. He laughed triumphantly. "So much for your proof!"

I shrugged. "I don't need it any more. The first part was authentic enough, but the real meat of it was fabricated. We constructed the rest of Longstaff's dialogue from other tapes loaned to us by Allman & Spinks. *You* were played by an actor friend of mine ..."

"But the sounds in the jacuzzi?"

"We just splashed around a little ... "

He was confused. "So it's still basically your word against mine?"

I hesitated but did not think it was yet time to mention the recording being made by Murdoch. " ... I also have the binder's knife you used to stab Stephen Gorton. It has your fingerprints on the handle."

"You're bluffing again," he said, but he was now totally disorientated.

"It's behind you on the bookshelves, next to the fishing books you were admiring."

He glanced back, saw the knife and took it down. It was not the same, of course, but it was impossible to tell the difference from the memory. He looked hopefully from the blade, to me. "What were we saying about it being your word against mine?"

I smiled. "Don't try it. I've got a shop full of customers, all potential witnesses. I could be out there in two or three strides, and I'd be back with one of the antique swords on display, so it would be a bit one-sided. Put the knife down, there's a good chap."

He did not argue, putting it down on a coffee-table between us; a tacit acceptance of defeat.

Ellen picked up the knife by the blade and studied it curiously. "Were his fingerprints really on the handle?" she asked.

"They are now."

"Good." Rounding on him, she made no effort to conceal her loathing. "You bastard! Why don't we still have the death penalty? If I had the guts I'd kill you myself."

Although he refused to meet her eyes, Farini was still in possession of his wits. "You're probably right – there's nothing I can say in my defence. But there's no way I can be convicted without 'Cintha being involved. No matter how much I swear she didn't know a thing, they'll match her to the fingerprints on the car … "

The knife handle had somehow found its way into Ellen's grip and I noticed that the muscles tightened instinctively. "Put it down!" I urged.

To my surprise, Ellen obeyed me. "I told you once before he was a shit, I wasn't wrong, was I?"

"I was stating a simple fact," Farini protested. "There's nothing to connect her with any of this – unless they get to me first."

Ellen's eyes found mine. "You're the only person who knows about the other links. If he is prepared to confess to killing Tony, is there any way you can leave Jacintha out of it?"

Conscious of Murdoch in the other room, surprisingly patient, I shook my head. "I can't speak for the police. They may not be too keen on going for a murder charge without a body. But they're already investigating David Morgan's death, and she is more directly involved in that than her father."

She cut me short. "I would do anything to save her – even get *him* off the hook. You said you were only bluffing when you asked for money before, but now *I'm* asking *you*. You stood to do well from Tony's pension fund, but between us there could be a real pension – for life ..."

She was a passionate, even ruthless woman, singleminded in her devotion; but surely love and loyalty were nothing to be ashamed of? I hesitated, giving rein to the conflicting thoughts that besieged my conscience, demanding attention. Morgan was the only person who merited my consideration and in my position he would have bowed to Ellen's wishes. I looked at the girl who had run him down. Her colour was returning, and with it her confidence. A shy, tremulous smile appeared on her lips that was hard to resist. But my own smile was as much at Ellen's unnecessary concern as it was for the girl's charm.

Jacintha could look after herself; indeed, it would be interesting to see how she fared with the professionals. That was Murdoch's problem from now on – I had a bookshop to run.